The Trouble With
Zinny Weston

AMY GOLDMAN KOSS

Dial Books for Young Readers
New York

Published by Dial Books for Young Readers
A member of Penguin Putnam Inc.
375 Hudson Street · New York, New York 10014

Copyright © 1998 by Amy Goldman Koss
All rights reserved
Designed by Pamela Darcy
Printed in the U.S.A. on acid-free paper
First Edition
1 3 5 7 9 10 8 6 4 2

Library of Congress Cataloging in Publication Data
Koss, Amy Goldman, date.
The trouble with Zinny Weston / Amy Goldman
Koss.—1st ed.
p.   cm.
Summary: Animal lover Ava feels torn about what she
should do when she hears that her best friend's mother
has drowned a raccoon in a garbage can.
ISBN 0-8037-2287-7 (trade)
[1. Animals—Treatment—Fiction. 2. Best friends—Fiction.
3. Friendship—Fiction.]   I. Title.   PZ7.K8527Rac
1998   [Fic]—dc21   97-28527   CIP   AC

To my dearly best beloveds,
Max and Harriet Goldman
and Mitchell, Emily, and Bennett Koss

And thanks to Dale Cohodes

Zinny Weston didn't come into the fifth grade clinging to the walls like most new kids. She didn't act all freaked and wormy. She even smiled.

Mrs. Hicks introduced Zinny to the class and then she called on me. "Ava, will you show Zinnia around today?"

I got up from my desk and walked toward Zinny while Mrs. Hicks said, "Tell her how we do things."

Zinny followed me to the back of the room and whispered, "So, how do you do things?"—perfectly imitating Mrs. Hicks's voice.

"We do things very badly," I said. "School policy—we do things badly, or we don't do them at all."

Zinny giggled with a little snort and from that exact moment we were friends.

"We have to hang our jackets and backpacks on these hooks," I said.

"And if we don't?" Zinny asked.

"Well, then they shoot us, of course," I explained.

She nodded as if that was reasonable and asked, "And what happens around here if you don't *use* a backpack?"

"Then they have to stick many, many sharp needles into your fingertips."

"Oh." Zinny shrugged. "Same as my old school."

When we went to the cafeteria and got in line for lunch, I made up terrible punishments for not emptying your lunch tray and for throwing away the silverware. "And if you forget your lunch money," I told her, "then they pull out all the hair on your head."

"Just your head?" she asked. "Well, that's a relief. At my old school they took our eyelashes too."

I laughed. "Then you'll like it here. Everybody is very nice. They don't even *touch* your eyelashes, unless you're late for P.E."

Then I heard Melinda's voice over my shoulder. "Too bad they're all out of gorilla food today. Guess you better check the rubbish bins out back."

My shoulders tensed, as always. I didn't look at Melinda, but I did glance at Zinny. She seemed confused for a second. Then, reaching for a banana, Zinny said, "Here's some."

I kept my eyes forward. Melinda got right up in my face and said, "It's your lucky day, Gorilla, a banana!"

I tried to ignore her and pushed my tray farther up the line. I felt Zinny look from Melinda to me and back again, still holding the banana.

"Too bad you got stuck being shown around by a gorilla," Melinda said to Zinny. "Did you get a good look at those hairy arms of hers? Her legs? How about those eyebrows?"

Zinny smiled very sweetly at Melinda and said, "Better a gorilla than a jackass." Everyone in line laughed, because they could tell Zinny meant Melinda. Zinny put the banana on her own tray and caught up with me in the line.

"Isn't she a peach?" Zinny said. I smiled—and breathed, realizing I'd been holding my breath. Zinny didn't say anything else about Melinda or the gorilla thing, so I didn't have to tell her that it had been going on for two months—practically the whole time I'd been at this school. Zinny and I just kept making up new things to laugh about.

When we went out for recess, she asked me if I jumped rope. "Not very well," I admitted.

"I'm not terrific at it either," Zinny said, "but I do know a few tricks. Wanna see?"

I said, "Sure."

Zinny grabbed a jumprope out of the pile of

balls and ropes. But instead of jumping with it, she wrapped it around her head like a turban with the two handles sticking out the top. I couldn't believe it. She'd done it so fast and it looked so funny! I laughed.

Zinny whisked the rope off her head and started twisting it around my head. Two girls in our class, Suki and Crystal, came over to watch. We were all laughing as Zinny made one strange headdress after another.

"I'm going to be a costume designer one day," Zinny said.

"Do one on me! Pretty please," Suki begged. So next Zinny made a big loopy hat on Suki. Crystal squeezed my arm and said, "Suki looks like a court jester! Don't you think it's a riot?"

Suki and Crystal had been in my class all along, but neither of them had ever talked to me before. Maybe they'd never noticed me, but more likely they'd been afraid that if they were nice to me Melinda would turn mean on them too.

"Me next! Me next!" Crystal squealed, squeezing my arm again. Zinny did a head wrap on Crystal, and we were all laughing so hard that it took a minute to notice that Melinda was scowling at us.

"Maybe we'll all get lucky and they'll hang themselves with that rope," Melinda said. A few kids snickered. "Hey, New Kid!" Melinda called. "Are you going to dress Gorilla up for the circus?

Maybe do a little organ grinding and pass the hat for handouts?"

Zinny whisked the jumprope off Crystal's head and quickly tied it into a lasso. She started twirling it over her head like a cowgirl, looking Melinda right in the eye.

"Anyone want to see me bring down a heifer?" Zinny called out, laughing. A few kids laughed along with Zinny. But most of us were silent, wondering what Melinda would do. We'd never seen anyone stand up to her before. I certainly had never defended myself against Melinda's gorilla taunts.

Melinda's eyes darted around. Then she stuck out her chin, poked her nose in the air, turned around, and walked stiffly toward the swings. That's all? I thought. Melinda just *walked away*? I couldn't believe it!

Zinny shrugged, then twisted the lasso into a ball. She threw it in the air and caught it, just as the bell rang for the end of recess. And Melinda suddenly shrank, in my mind, from being Mighty Melinda—the poisonous, fanged, all-powerful dragon with a forty-foot wingspan—down to a tiny, annoying flea.

Zinny flicked a note onto my desk after lunch, and I giggled before I even unfolded it. She and I passed funny notes in class all afternoon. I learned that she even lived in my subdivision! By the end of the day all we had to do was look at each other to burst out laughing.

We walked home from school together and talked about how weird it was that every house in the whole subdivision was so new. "It's like we are Eve and Eve, the first two girls on Earth!" Zinny said.

"I just moved here before school started," I told her, "from a cruddy condo apartment in town. We had a drummer living downstairs with zero sense of rhythm."

"Nice," Zinny said.

"He practiced constantly—except when he was screaming at his girlfriend."

"I bet you miss all that," she said. "I know I plan to miss falling on the ice and gagging on frozen wind. I already miss having lips so chapped, they crack and bleed."

"Siberia?" I asked.

"Chicago," she answered. "My dad got transferred here for his job. This isn't how I pictured California."

"Me neither," I said, "and I've lived in California all my life."

We walked past one of those miserable new trees propped up with sticks and rope, and I said, "I know how that thing feels."

Zinny struck a pose, imitating the tree, all strangled and shocked looking. "It's our tree, we have high hopes for it," she said, snorting when she laughed.

"This is your house? You live here?" I asked. And that's how we discovered that if we cut through two backyards, at an angle, we were at each other's houses!

All the houses in our subdivision were identical except that some were still being built and others already had lawns and shrubs. I went inside with Zinny and met her mom. It felt spooky to be in a house exactly like ours, but with different furniture and wallpaper. Theirs was fancier and cleaner, even though they'd just moved in. At my house there were still unpacked boxes to trip over, but it looked as if the Westons had lived here forever.

I called home to tell my mom not to worry, that I'd gone to a friend's house. She was so happy that you'd think I'd won the lottery. I guess Mom had noticed that I hadn't exactly made a ton of friends in the new school.

Mrs. Weston made us each an afternoon snack of a mini-muffin and a glass of milk—period. The three of us sat on stools at their kitchen counter, which was just like ours only somehow, completely different. We had this conversation:

Mrs. Weston: "What do your parents do, Ava?"

Me: "They have a clinic in town called Fins, Fangs, Feathers, and Fur. They're veterinarians."

Mrs. Weston: "Animal veterinarians? Both of them? Your mother too?"

Me: "Yes."

Mrs. Weston: "How interesting." Her tone of voice didn't sound interested, though. It sounded polite.

Zinny and I went up to her room, which was everything and nothing like mine. Zinny asked me if I had any brothers or sisters.

I shook my head. "I have some pets, though," I said. "I have a German shepherd named Ralph and a lizard named Rock. I had two lizards, Rock and Roll, but Roll died. I might get another roommate for Rock, but maybe not, because some lizards fight, and you never can tell until you put them together."

"Lizards? Fighting lizards?" Zinny squealed. "You're kidding, right?"

"No," I said. "And I have two lovebirds named Kiss and Hug, two hermit crabs, Michelle and Shelly, and two rats who we call 'The Boys' although their names are really Pete and Re-Pete."

"You have rats? On purpose?" Zinny asked, squinting at me.

"They're very sweet," I assured her. "You'll like them."

"No I won't," Zinny said. "The thought of rats running around . . ."

"They're in a cage in my bedroom."

"Well that takes care of my ever sleeping over," Zinny sighed. "But that's okay—you'll sleep here! You want to?"

"Sure!" I said. "But maybe one day you'll change your mind about rats."

"And dogs?" Zinny asked. "And lizards? And what were the other ones—lobsters? Clams?"

"Crabs."

"Oh, crabs! I love them!" Zinny said. "Especially soft-shelled crabs—with butter. Does that count?"

"No, that doesn't count, and neither do crab-cakes," I said.

"Yummmm!" Zinny said. "I love those too. It's funny, because my sister, Rose, is allergic to crab. All shellfish, in fact. If she eats one shrimp, she blows up like a balloon. Actually, she's allergic to everything. One time, when she was a baby, before I was born—"

"I always wanted a big sister," I interrupted.

"Not this big. Rose doesn't even live with us. She goes to college up north and I hardly see her."

"Oh," I said.

"Anyway," Zinny continued, "when Rose was

little, she played with someone's cat and she turned blue and couldn't breathe and had to be rushed to the hospital!"

"Wow!" I said.

"My mom has told me the Rose-to-the-hospital story so many times that I practically remember it better than my own trip to the hospital to have my appendix out. My mom thinks cats should be illegal. Dogs too. She says all animals are filthy and carry disease."

"I don't think your mom and my mom are going to be pals," I said.

"Your mom the *vet?*" Zinny asked, and laughed.

It didn't seem so important, right then, that I was an animal lover and Zinny wasn't. But boy, was I wrong.

I sat eating breakfast one Sunday morning about a month after I met Zinny. My parents were reading the newspaper at the table. I saw my dad's hand snake out from behind the paper and grope for his coffee cup.

I was watching the sunshine streaking through the living room windows. My dog Ralph had shredded the curtains trying to get to the mailman. Seeing the tatters gave me an idea.

"We should take those curtains down," I said.

Dad grunted.

I tried again. "Those curtains are pretty ugly, Mom."

"They didn't used to be," my mom answered, frowning at Ralph.

"Well, they are ugly now. So can I have them?" I asked.

"What for?"

"For just stuff. For me and Zinny."

There was no answer so I added, "I'll clean up all Ralph's poop in the yard if you'll let me have the curtains. Please?"

My mom put down her newspaper and said, "It's a deal."

I ran into the backyard and scooped the poop, then washed my hands and raced into the living room to help my mom take the curtains down. I stuffed them into a garbage bag to haul over to Zinny's house.

During the month I'd known Zinny, my feet had learned to automatically follow the path across the yards to her house. But it was different lugging the bag of heavy curtains. By the time I got to her house, I was beat.

"Hey," Zinny said, opening the door. She always says "hey," instead of hello.

"Hey, yourself," I panted. "You want to be a world-famous costume designer, right?"

"Right," Zinny said, peeking around me at the garbage bag.

"Well, now I can see if you're as good with cloth as you are with jumpropes."

Zinny's face lit up as she dove into the bag. "You be my model!" she said. "Put your arms out." I did and Zinny began draping the old curtains over and around me. It made me giggle when she went near my armpits.

"I don't think models can be ticklish," Zinny said.

"I'm not going to be a model," I said. "I'm going to be a singer, and singers can be as ticklish as they like. Temperamental too. In fact, I should be throwing tantrums while you work, to make it more realistic for you."

"Great!" Zinny said. "You rant and I'll design— the perfect team! You're so totally famous and moody that you won't allow anyone to do your costumes but me. Absolutely no one. Other costume designers are always begging you to let them dress you—but you say, 'Never! There will never be anyone but Zinnia Weston!'"

"Either Zinnia Weston costumes me, or I go onstage naked!" I squealed. "Tonight I'm singing a huge concert for the queen of England, and a few princes, and a bunch of other royalty. We are flying over the ocean to get there, in my private jet, right?"

"Right," Zinny agreed. "And we're almost there, but you've just gotten into one of those *moods* of yours."

"And I've decided that I hate all my old costumes and you have to come up with something new before we land," I said.

"Not just new," Zinny said, wrapping me in a cocoon of curtain fabric, "but something so truly amazing that the queen will take one look and make us honorary princesses."

The phone rang. Mr. Weston answered it and called out, "Ava, your mother's on the phone."

I trailed yards of cloth into the den to get the phone. My mom said it was time to leave for the shelter and to come on home. I asked if I could bring Zinny with me and Mom said, "Sure."

I usually looked forward all week to Sundays— that's the day my parents volunteer at the animal shelter, and I go along with whichever one goes that week. But now I hated to leave Zinny. I started unwinding myself from her costume and said, "Sorry, I gotta run."

"The animal thing?" Zinny asked.

"Yeah, the shelter," I said. "You want to come?"

"Sure," Zinny said, looking sadly at the heap of curtains.

Zinny asked her mom if she could go with me. Mrs. Weston seemed doubtful.

I explained that the shelter was a big compound out in the desert where people brought wild animals that had been hurt. "My folks and other vets fix them up and then release them into nature," I told her. "There are farm animals too, that Animal Protection confiscates from people with illegal livestock in the city. They make up our petting zoo."

Zinny's mom looked blank.

"Animal Protection is the county animal regulation police," I explained. "We also have exotic animals that people don't want as pets anymore, like bears and tigers."

I should have noticed that Mrs. Weston was turning pale, but I didn't. I went on, "People think animals like that will make cool pets. Then after they have them declawed and have all their teeth yanked out, they decide they aren't such cool pets after all, and they bring them in. We can't release them, so unless a zoo takes them, they stay on forever. So do the wild animals that can't be released. There's an owl that can't fly, and a blind coyote, and about three hundred and fifty other animals."

"Perhaps Zinnia can go with you some other time," Mrs. Weston said. But her face said *"Never!"* as if I'd asked if Zinny could join me for a swim in a pit of venomous snakes.

So I left Zinny and went off to the shelter with my dad. Dad and I spent the half-hour drive playing Twenty Questions. When we got there, he headed for the hospital bungalow. I went into the office next door.

Rita Taylor was at the desk. She was, as always, perfectly neat and perfectly polite and busy with some useful task. That's ever-helpful Rita. She was only two years older than me, but she acted like a grown-up hiding in a kid's body.

"Good morning, Ava," she said, like an old lady. "How are you?"

Her parents are the vets that run the shelter, and they've been best friends with my parents since the dawn of humankind. I've known Rita forever, so I know she's always been perfect. She made her bed every morning and loved to help with chores. She was always the class president and every other parent-pleasing thing.

My parents thought she was great. *Her* parents thought she was great. Even her whiny, tattle-telling little brother, Eli, thought she was great. I was perhaps the only person on Earth who thought Rita Taylor was a bossy pain in the butt.

When she acted too, too perfect, I told myself that she was secretly a puppet—a girl Pinocchio—not a real kid. That made it easier for me to stand her goody-goodyness, and it somehow made it easier to be her friend.

Anyway, I was in the shelter office with Rita when Mike, from Animal Protection, walked in with a box. He lowered it so we could see what was inside.

"Another abused Easter bunny," Mike said. "This one lasted longer than most. The owners went on vacation and left her outside in her cage. No food, no water. The gardener found her."

Rita got out the ledger book as if this was just

another animal to process. But when that rabbit looked up at me with her sad, dark eyes, I instantly fell in love.

I guess my feelings showed because Rita said, in her older-and-wiser voice, "Ava, try to control your emotions. You cannot go wild over every unfortunate creature that comes in here."

She was referring to The Boys. A few months back I'd snatched them out of the feeder tank, where they were waiting to be food for the rat-eating snakes and owls and eagles.

"I don't go *wild* over every animal," I said. "Just this one." I looked at that sweet, honey-colored rabbit and named her Honey Bunny.

I held Honey while my dad examined her and gave her two shots. When I told him I needed to keep her, he said, "I don't want a lot of weeping hysterics if she dies on you."

"Nope. No hysterics," I promised.

I sat on the couch in the office, holding Honey wrapped up in a towel on my lap. Rita was sitting at the desk, looking efficient, although there was no work to do.

I stroked Honey's fur. "Maybe Zinny will actually like a rabbit," I said. "She's my new friend who I was telling you about. Remember?"

Rita nodded without looking up from her pretend work.

"Well, Zinny is really great and funny and everything, but she's entirely grossed out by animals," I said. "Her mom is too. They both think animals are filthy and carry disease. I need to work on her."

"It takes all kinds of people to make the world," Rita said, in her Miss Priss voice.

"Like today," I continued. "I wanted Zinny to come out here with me and she acted like she wanted to—but really, I think she was relieved that her mom wouldn't let her come. I'm not sure."

"I, personally, think good friends should have good things in common," Rita said.

"Everything we have in common is *good*," I said.

As my dad and Honey and I were leaving, Rita's parents stood around, watching us go. "Ava's going to make a zoo out of that new house of yours," Rita's dad called out.

My dad just waved and got into the car.

I called Rita's parents the Perfect Taylors. Since their daughter was so perfect, they thought of themselves as the world's experts on raising kids. They always had plenty of advice on how to shape me up. I was glad my dad ignored them this time.

3

My mom showed me how to give Honey her antibiotics with an eyedropper. "Watch out for those teeth," my mom said, but she didn't have to say that because Honey Bunny didn't even try to bite me. Mom also showed me how to clean Honey's sore feet. Her paws were so swollen and infected from standing in that filthy cage, she'd already lost two toenails.

I searched my brain for songs about bunny rabbits and sang every one I could think of to Honey while I treated her feet: "Here comes Peter Cottontail" and "Mr. Rabbit, Mr. Rabbit, your ears are mighty long. Yes indeed, they're put on wrong. . . ." She was remarkably brave, and it really did seem that she liked my voice.

I kept Honey in my bedroom and woke up about five times that first night to make sure she was okay. In the morning Zinny knocked at my front door and yelled, "Hurry, slowpoke, we'll be late."

I grabbed my backpack and went out front to meet her. On the way to school I told her about Honey Bunny.

"When I lived in Chicago," Zinny said, "I had a bunny-fur jacket. It was really cold there, you know."

I got chills thinking about my Honey as a jacket. I tried to rub the goose bumps off my arms. Zinny didn't notice.

"It used to shed like crazy," Zinny continued. "My mom made me sit forward in the car so it wouldn't get all over the seats, but I *loved* that jacket."

"Well, I *love* Honey Bunny!" I said.

Zinny covered her mouth. "Oops. Sorry," she said.

I told her it was okay. Then I told myself to just shove the image of Zinny wearing a Honey Bunny jacket into a bottom drawer of my brain—and bury it under all the things I liked about her.

That whole day at school I worried about Honey being left all alone in the house. Well, not exactly alone—she had Ralph and The Boys and the other animals, but no *human* to pet her and sing bunny songs to her.

Finally the school day ended. I rushed Zinny

out of the building and tried to get her to hurry to my house. When we got there, my dad was setting up a rabbit hutch in the backyard.

"Is Honey all right?" I called to him.

"Fine as sunshine," he called back.

I ran inside. Zinny waited while I put Ralph in my parents' room, because Zinny is afraid of him. Then I dashed into my room, dragging Zinny behind me. There was Honey. She was not exactly as fine as sunshine, but at least she was still alive.

Zinny opened the windows in my room. Then she stood with her arms clamped tight at her sides, keeping her distance from The Boys' cage. I gently lifted Honey out of her box and petted her. I held her out for Zinny to see, but Zinny shrank back. Oh, well.

I told Zinny that I had to clean Honey's infected feet.

"That's way too gross for me!" Zinny said. "I'll wait outside."

When I was done, I put Honey back in her box to rest and then went out to find Zinny and my dad. They were in the backyard trying to name all the kinds of houses in the world. Lighthouse, igloo, treehouse, thatched hut, houseboat . . . it was fun. Maybe Zinny hated my pets, but I was glad she liked my dad at least.

Honey Bunny got a little stronger and her feet got a little better every day. My mom told me to start taking her outside for a half hour a day so she'd get used to the world again. It was nice sitting under the tree with Honey on my lap. Sometimes I'd rock with her on the hammock and sing to her. Zinny said that Honey was going to be the most musical of voiceless creatures.

When Honey could hop without pain, my folks said it was time to move her to the hutch. I worried that she would be scared or lonely out in the back-yard all alone. Maybe it would remind her of her terrible past, when she was trapped in that filthy cage with no food or water.

Zinny thought I was bonkers, but she came up with the perfect idea the day I put Honey in her hutch. "Why don't you ask your folks if we can camp out in the backyard tonight? We could sleep right next to the hutch and baby-sit your rabbit."

I thought it was brilliant.

My folks made us promise that we wouldn't keep the whole neighborhood awake all night. Then they said okay. My dad hauled our tent out of the garage and set it up next to the hutch. Zinny and I spent the rest of the day arranging our camp, packing our provisions and pretending we were on a safari.

When the sun went down, we sat on a pile of

sleeping bags and blankets, eating Fig Newtons and making shadows on the tent walls with our flashlights. Then Zinny put on a scary, low voice and said, "Ava, did I ever tell you about the two girls who were camping in a little blue tent, just like this one?"

I felt the hairs on my arms tingle. "Nope," I said.

"It was a particularly dark night, way out in the desert," Zinny said slowly. "No stars, and only a thin toenail clipping of a moon. It was so dark that they could barely even make out the few cacti that stood around like cowboys with their hands up. The girls had put their little blue tent up far, far from everyone and everything—or so they thought!"

I squealed. I loved scary stories. When Zinny got to the part about the escaped convict who snuck up on the girls, I screamed. Zinny screamed too, and then we were laughing and screaming so much that when my dad stuck his head into the tent opening we both jumped about ten feet in the air.

"Girls!" he hissed. "Cut it out! Go to sleep!"

When he left, it was my turn to tell a horror story about two girls, just like us, who didn't know they'd pitched their tent on ancient sacred burial grounds—on the very night of a ghost celebration.

I freaked both of us out so badly that we had to

grab our blankets and run inside. We slept on the living room floor, with all the lights on.

When Honey's feet were healed and her appetite was back, my parents and I talked about what to do with her. If we let her loose, she would be in danger from coyotes, hawks, cars, and maybe snakes, but my dad felt that a short, natural life was better than a long, dreary one in a hutch.

Mom said, "I don't know. I think a bunny with a full belly and nothing to fear is a happy bunny. Maybe Honey doesn't need adventure or freedom."

Dad peered over his reading glasses. "What crime did this rabbit commit to deserve life imprisonment in solitary confinement, twenty-four-seven?"

"What's twenty-four-seven?" I asked.

"That's prison talk for twenty-four hours a day, seven days a week," he said. "Eating processed pellets. Never to bound free across the yard, only able to manage a few cramped steps behind bars."

Mom rolled her eyes, but we agreed to take the chance and set Honey free. I secretly feared that Honey was so tame and fearless now with people that someone else in the neighborhood would catch her and keep her.

When my dad pried the door off Honey's hutch,

she did not leap out with a song in her heart, thrilled to be free. She cowered at the back of the hutch, scared to death. She was still crouching there when I went to bed.

I rushed out the second I woke up the next morning and found her hopping around outside her hutch, nibbling grass. I was glad that she'd decided to come out of her hutch but hadn't run away, and relieved that she'd made it through the night without getting eaten. I gave her treats so she'd know where her home was.

Honey mostly stayed put, napping under the hammock and watching butterflies. And when she did go off on her secret bunny adventures, it was never for too long. I wondered where she went, and then I found out.

Saturday is "family day" at our house. No school, no clinic, no shelter. It's the one day we all sleep late. But early one Saturday morning we were awakened by the doorbell. I got there first and found Zinny's dad, Mr. Weston, on the porch, holding Honey out by her delicate ears, which you're never supposed to do.

Honey's feet were kicking wildly. Her eyes were enormous. I took her in my arms and could feel her heart racing with terror.

My dad stood behind me, tying his robe.

"That," Mr. Weston said, pointing a disgusted finger at Honey, "ate my wife's prize petunias."

"Sorry," my dad said, not sounding very sorry. "That must have been very traumatic for your wife."

This made Zinny's dad madder. "She had some very rare varieties. They don't come cheap, you know," he said.

My dad raised one eyebrow, in a rude sort of way, like the price of petunias was a joke. He didn't say anything. He certainly didn't say he'd pay for the petunias.

Now Mr. Weston looked really steamed and said, "I will not bring that rabbit back here next time. If it comes on my property one more time, it will be the last." Then he turned and marched away. My dad slammed the door.

"How could you do that?" I screamed. "That's Zinny's father!"

"Don't take that tone of voice with me," he said in a huff.

"Zinny is my best friend!" I shrieked.

"And this is your rabbit!"

I stomped out back with Honey and held her until she was calm. I couldn't sing any bunny songs, though, because I was too busy wondering how I would ever face Zinny. Whichever dad was right, mine had sure acted ridiculous. Rude and snotty and ridiculous! I wanted to be loyal to Dad—he was my *dad* after all. But did he have to act like such a brat? Even if he didn't see the major big deal about petunias, Zinny's parents planted petunias because they wanted petunias—and if people want petunias, they should have petunias. And if people go naming their kids Rose and Zinnia, they probably *really* like flowers.

Monday morning Zinny picked me up for school and the first thing I noticed was that she was wearing a dress that looked very familiar. Zinny twirled in front of me, giggling.

"It's the curtains!" I shrieked. "You're brilliant!"

"I know, I know." Zinny laughed with a little snort. "There's still lots left. Want me to make one for you?"

We walked together, talking about dresses and costumes and curtains. I didn't mention Honey Bunny or petunias or our dads and neither did she. Not one single word.

After the Honey Bunny fathers' fight, I was really
surprised when Mrs. Weston got it into her head to
have a fishpond built in their backyard. Not just a
hole in the mud, but a beautiful thing that took
lots of planning and a slew of designers and con-
tractors. I thought maybe Zinny and her parents
were changing their minds about animals.

Suki and Crystal and I were all up in Zinny's
room playing Monopoly. All board games give me
the bored teary yawns, but Monopoly is the worst.
I can never remember what's what and who's who
and I can't seem to care. But for some bizarre rea-
son, it's Suki's favorite game. Crystal pointed out
Zinny's window and said, "The next time that guy
bends over, I bet his pants are going to fall all the
way off."

We all ran to the window and looked down into Zinny's yard at a man digging a hole for the fishpond. We laughed until we couldn't breathe, watching his pants slip down his big old butt.

"Gross!" Zinny squealed.

"Crystal, I'll give you my house on Boardwalk if his pants fall off," Suki said, trying to get us back to the Monopoly game. "And if his pants stay on, you have to give me your hotel on Marvin Gardens."

"No way," said Crystal. "I get your hotel on St. Charles *and* your house on Boardwalk."

"He's leaving," Zinny said. "Let's go look at the hole he dug."

"But what about the game?" Suki whined.

"We can finish later," Zinny said. I was relieved.

We went outside and tried to jump clear across the hole, which we said was bottomless quicksand. All of us fell in and sank to our deaths except Crystal. She's a great jumper. She's also good at cartwheels and flips. She wants to be a cheerleader.

The man with the slipping pants came back to Zinny's the next day and finished digging the hole and laying the pipes. Then another guy came to pour the cement. He was nice. He told Zinny and me knock-knock jokes while we stood around watching him. And he called us "A to Z." "Ava to Zinnia. Get it?" he asked. We got it. After him came the tile man. Or was the electrician next?

Anyway, the fishpond cost a lot of money, and it took weeks of work before it was *exactly* the way Zinny's mom wanted it.

"The really big deal," I said to Zinny, "is that those fish are going to be your first pets! I think it's exciting."

"It's not like I'm going to swim with them," Zinny said. "Or teach them to fetch or anything. They're going to be fish! More like decorations, I think, than *pets*."

"Yeah, but they'll be alive," I said.

When the big day came, Zinny insisted that I come along to the tropical fish store. On the way Mrs. Weston made it clear that not just any old fish would do. She needed giant, fancy, incredibly expensive, ornamental Japanese koi for her fishpond.

Zinny and I stood together, looking at all the fat koi swimming around in a massive aquarium. Zinny's mom stood back a bit, being very careful not to touch anything. And especially not to touch the sweaty-looking tropical fish store man.

"How about that white one with the gold face?" I said, just to get things started.

The tropical fish store man swirled his net in the tank. "This one?" he asked.

I looked at Zinny. She shrugged. "Come on, Zinny, you gotta pick," I said. "They're your pets!"

Zinny made a nervous, cross-eyed, goofy face, then peered into the tank some more.

"So?" said the fish man. "Which?"

"Just give me ten healthy ones," Mrs. Weston said.

The fish man caught a pretty red- and gold-flecked koi and slid it into a plastic bag. It was so huge that it needed a whole bag of its own. He held the bag out. Neither Zinny nor her mom reached for it, so I took it.

With a great deal of swirling and splashing the fish man bagged the next few koi. When I was holding all I could, Zinny put out a tentative hand to take the next one. She squealed, holding the fish in its bag of water at arm's length.

When Zinny's hands were full, the fish man held out a bag to her mom. Mrs. Weston looked positively squeamish and said, "Don't you have a box?"

I tried to keep things cheerful, but it wasn't easy. At last Zinny's mom slipped out her gold credit card and paid the man, and we were on our way back to their house with two big sloshy boxes of fish. I suspected I would be the one to put the fish in their new pond—and I was right.

The fishpond had turned out very pretty, with a twinkly little fountain and decorated tiles. Around it the gardeners had planted yellow daisies. Lights shone on it at night like a fairy castle. Once I'd plopped in the koi, everyone was happy.

Zinny and I tried to name the fish. "If there's a way to tell boy fish from girl fish, it sure isn't obvious," Zinny said. "Unless maybe you're a fish."

"Well, not to hurt anyone's feelings, let's call that gold speckled one Sam, for Samantha or Samuel," I said.

"That whitish one will be Ball," Zinny said, "for Football or Basketball."

I added, "There's Chicken, for Chicken Soup or Chicken Pox."

The koi swam around so much, we couldn't keep them straight. By the time each fish had about four names, we were laughing so hard we had to give up. We decided to call them The Wet Pets when we talked about them at all—which wasn't often.

Then a few days later Zinny's mom went out to look at her pond and three fish were gone. Everyone was mystified. How could fish disappear?

I was there the next morning when Mrs. Weston discovered two more koi missing without a trace.

"Wow! Look at her go!" Zinny said. "It's a Wet Pet fish frenzy!"

I looked out the window at Mrs. Weston thrashing in the daisies next to the fishpond. She was uprooting whole plants and throwing them around. Clumps of dirt flew.

"What's she looking for—fish bodies?" I asked.

"Footprints? Clues?" Zinny giggled. "A ransom note?"

We could hear Zinny's mom muttering to herself. Her face was bright red. It's always interesting to see grown-ups go wacko, but this was particularly interesting because Mrs. Weston is usually so calm. Her blond hair moves perfectly with her head, like a helmet. Her makeup is always just so. Her clothes never wrinkle, and she wears high heels every day without complaining that her feet hurt.

My mom isn't like that. My mom has long fuzzy hair that's always springing out of her pony tail. She says she's going gray, but really she's going black and white in stripes like a skunk. Mom's clothes have a mismatched look and she never wears hard shoes.

Our two dads, Zinny's and mine, are different too. Mr. Weston wears a suit and tie every day, and even on weekends his shirt is tucked in and his hair is combed. My dad's only comb is his fingers and he has a straggly red beard that holds bits of lunch. He wears his lab coat over cutoff blue jeans, and he usually wears sandals with socks.

That's why Mrs. Weston's tantrum in the daisies was so interesting. Actually, I thought it was a good sign. First Zinny's mom got real live fish and had a beautiful home built for them, and then she cared that they disappeared.

On the way to school the next day Zinny said, "The mystery of the missing Wet Pets has been solved! Last night my mom flicked on the pond lights and started grunting like this." Zinny grunted three times. "Then my dad raced outside, in his pj's, yelling his head off."

I asked, "What was it?"

"Guess."

"The koi were abducted by aliens?" I asked.

"Nope."

"Airlifted to Marine Land?"

"Eaten by a *raccoon!*" Zinny said, as if a raccoon was the strangest possible creature to find in your yard. As if it was a boa constrictor or a dinosaur. "This big old raccoon was dipping into our pond, chomping away at our fish like chips out of a bowl! My dad scared it away."

We both laughed until Zinny said, "But you know, koi are way too expensive to be *raccoon* food!" She shuddered at the word *raccoon*.

When I said the raccoon had a right to eat too, Zinny shot me a look that meant she thought I was wacko. "He doesn't have a right to eat *our* koi in *our* backyard!" Zinny said. "Let him go live in the woods or something."

"He *was* living in the woods," I said. "Then *we* came along and built houses and fishponds in *his* backyard! He probably thinks the koi are your way of saying, 'Sorry for the mess we made of your land.' Maybe he thought the fish were like rent payment."

"He doesn't *think* anything," Zinny said. "He's a *raccoon!* A dumb animal! A destructive, dumb animal that probably carries the plague and rabies and who knows what else."

By this time we were in front of the school. Suki and Crystal came up to us and we changed the subject. But that raccoon versus koi thing drifted through my mind all day. I should have known then that there was raccoon trouble ahead.

5

The next day Mr. Draper, the music teacher, gave me a huge solo to sing in the Spring Program. It was going to have an American folk song theme, and he asked me if I'd like to sing all three verses of "Sweet Betsy from Pike" by myself, with the rest of the class only coming in on the refrain. No one else got a part that big!

Zinny knows that I want to be a singer some day, more than anything, and Zinny is the kind of friend who is happy for you when you're happy. At school, in front of everyone, I had to act like it was no big deal, but when Zinny and I were walking home together I didn't have to pretend anymore.

"Probably there will be a talent scout in the audience," Zinny said, "someone's uncle or something. He'll come in bored stiff. Our first few songs nearly put him in a coma—and then—it's time for 'Sweet Betsy from Pike'! You sing the first line. . . ."

"He's really rich and handsome. And his whole job is to make singers famous," I added.

Zinny nodded, then said, "He hears you!" She stopped walking to imitate the talent scout, making herself look alert—like Ralph when he hears a thump. "'What an incredible voice!' he says. He wasn't paying attention before, so he doesn't know which kid sang that gorgeous solo. Then it's time for your second verse. Ah ha! He sees you!"

I shrieked.

"Now he's practically jumping out of his seat. When you sing the third verse, he cannot believe his ears! 'It's the voice of my dreams! The voice I've been waiting all my life to hear! I must make that girl a star!'"

"But," I said, "he looks at me in that dumb white blouse and black skirt and says, 'She'll need just exactly the right costume designer. Someone amazing . . .'"

Zinny bowed low and said, "Zinnia Weston, at your service."

Soon we were in front of her house, snorting and laughing. We went inside to get something to eat, still giggling. Mrs. Weston had laid out two bananas and a bag of popcorn for us. Zinny stuck the popcorn in the microwave and I peeled a banana. I was leaning against the kitchen counter, waiting for the popcorn to pop, when I looked out the window toward the fishpond. I saw Zinny's mom outside supervising the gardeners. I guess she was having them replant the daisies she'd uprooted. Next to Mrs. Weston I saw a cage. Not a regular cage; it looked like a trap.

"What's that for?" I asked, pointing at the trap.

"For the alien abductor who airlifted our koi to Marine Land," she said.

The banana I was eating turned gross and gooey in my mouth. I wanted to spit it out, but of course I didn't.

"What will your parents do with it if they catch it?" I asked.

"Airlift it to Disneyland?" Zinny asked. "Mickey and Minnie Mouse would love a raccoon. It would be a whole wacky rodent reunion."

I wished just this once, Zinny would give me a straight answer. "Raccoons aren't rodents," I said quietly.

I turned my back on the trap and watched Zinny burn her fingers opening the popcorn bag. She hopped around doing a hot-finger dance, as only Zinny could.

I watched my best friend clown around and thought—okay, her parents are weird, and I don't particularly like or understand them, but then I hardly understand *any* adults. And since when are kids to blame for their parents doing weird things—like wearing sandals with socks or setting raccoon traps?

Back home I tried to ask my dad about traps. "I was over at the Westons' just now . . ." I began.

"Picking petunias?" he asked.

So I dropped the subject. My dad obviously hadn't forgotten the Honey Bunny petunia incident. The last thing I wanted was to make my folks dislike Zinny's folks any more than they already seemed to. I suspected that if my dad knew that the Westons had set a trap for a raccoon, he would freak.

After dinner my parents and I were out in the backyard and I decided to try again. My lizard, Rock, was curled up in my pocket while I cleaned his cage. Pete, the rat, waited on my dad's shoulder while Re-Pete got his toenails clipped. My mom was drinking coffee and staring at the weeds.

I used my most casual voice. "Remember when that coyote ate Bob's cat in the old neighborhood?" (How could they forget? There had been tufts of fur all over the front yard of our apartment building.) "Did Bob do anything about it?" I asked.

"Like what?" my dad said, switching Pete for Re-Pete.

"Well, I dunno, set a coyote trap or anything?"

"A little late for that, don't you think?" my dad said.

"Well, would he have," I asked, "like if he had another cat and didn't want the same thing to happen again?"

"He could," Dad said.

"Would he just buy one at the hardware store or what?"

"He'd call Animal Protection," my mom said, "and they'd come out and set a Havahart—that's a live trap. Then they'd come back and pick it up when the coyote was caught."

"Then what?" I asked, as if I didn't care.

"The Animal Protection guys would drive the coyote up into the hills and let it go."

"So Bob couldn't just buy a trap and do it himself?"

"Bob? Pay for something out of his own pocket when he could get it for free?" My dad laughed.

"Animal Protection—your tax dollars at work," Mom added.

So that was that. The king and queen of animal lovers didn't think there was anything wrong with traps.

While Zinny French-braided my hair during recess the next day, she asked if I thought Jason

Treadwell was cute, which I do not. I asked if she did and she said I was batty, which we both knew meant *yes*.

Zinny, Crystal, Suki, and I had a watermelon seed spitting contest after school, which was fun. Zinny can't really spit at all—every seed just sort of drooled down her chin—but Suki could shoot them halfway to Tarzana.

"You're a true spit artist," Zinny told Suki. "This could lead to a brilliant future."

"Especially if you could do it on a unicycle while juggling raw eggs," I added.

"You two are always so sarcastic," Suki said. But we just laughed.

The next day, Saturday, Zinny called to say she had to get dressed up to go to some kind of country club event with her parents.

My parents lay around, reading and eating breakfast in bed. Every now and then one of them would brush crumbs off their sheets and say, "We really should get up and *do* something," but they didn't budge. I was bored out of my gourd.

Finally, after I'd been nagging them for hours, they dragged themselves out of bed and threw food in the picnic basket. We drove to the park, where my parents spread their blanket and lolled around eating and reading and telling me to go play and stop fidgeting. My dad looked over his reading glasses at me and said, "People who are bored are so boring." Family day.

But here's what happened when we got home: Suki called me on the phone and asked me if I'd talked to Zinny.

"Not since morning," I answered.

"Then you don't know," Suki said.

"Don't know what?"

"About the raccoon and all."

"Raccoon and all what?"

"Maybe I shouldn't tell you. . . ."

She was starting to drive me bonkers. "Suki! What is it?"

"Well," Suki paused, "I heard my mom say that Zinny's mom caught a raccoon in a trap, put the trap in a garbage can, then put the garden hose in the can and filled it with water—raccoon and all. Isn't that gross?"

When Suki told me this, I went blank in my brain—as if my head was full of white feathers. Then I pictured the trap in the garbage can, the raccoon's heart thumping like mad, his little brain trying to figure out what was going on. The water getting gradually deeper and deeper and that raccoon scrambling to keep his nose above water until he couldn't anymore, and drowned.

I don't remember saying good-bye or anything

else to Suki. I don't remember hanging up. I didn't cry, but I could feel my mouth opening and closing like a giant fish. I suddenly felt filthy and got into the shower. I stood under the hot water, wondering if Zinny knew what her mom had done. Had she been there? Waiting around the garbage can, while Mrs. Weston held the hose? Did Zinny try to stop her? Or did they make small talk and tell jokes, while the raccoon scrambled higher in the trap, gasping for air?

I made the water even hotter and scrubbed my body until my skin hurt. Then I got out and brushed and brushed my teeth, remembering the banana that had gone gooey and bitter in my mouth when I'd seen the trap at Zinny's.

I convinced myself that Zinny must have been at school or somewhere when the murder took place, and she couldn't have known anything about it—at least not at the time.

When I thought I appeared normal in the mirror, I went looking for my dad. I found him rocking in the hammock in the backyard with Ralph lying on the ground next to him.

I knelt down to pet Ralph and said, "Dad? We put flea collars on Ralph to kill his fleas because dogs are more important than fleas, right?"

"Important? What do you mean by important?" he said.

"Well, you know what I mean. . . . People put

out snail poison because snails eat their flowers. . . . They think that flowers are more important than snails. . . ."

"We don't," Dad said.

"Well, we kill mosquitoes," I said, losing track of
what I was saying. "And we wear leather shoes and
eat meat . . ."

"And we will, no doubt, have to answer for that
in the great by and by." Dad squinted at me, then
said, "Is this a riddle, or are we talking about something here? Is it that father-daughter, meaning-
of-life thing?"

"No," I said, no longer sure what my question
was. I knew one thing, and that was that I couldn't
tell my dad what Suki said that Zinny's mom did
to that raccoon.

I hugged Ralph, pressing my face into the thick
fur around his neck. I wondered if this whole
"which is more important" thing—raccoons or
fish, bunnies or petunias, fleas or dogs—was just
silly to everyone but me. I stood up to walk away.

"Did I miss something here?" my dad called after me, sounding concerned. "Was this an important conversation?"

"No, Dad, it's nothing," I said, and headed back
inside.

When I came into my bedroom, The Boys rushed
to the door of their cage, climbing over each other.

I opened the door and they squirmed out. Pete crawled up my chest to sniff tickly rat secrets in my ear. Re-Pete climbed my arm and poked his whiskery nose in my armpit. Thank goodness for rats.

I called Suki. "Suki, it's Ava. Could you do me a favor?"

"What?"

"Well, could you *not* tell Zinny that you told me about her mom and the raccoon? You know . . . the part about . . . you know."

"Oops," said Suki.

"What oops?" I said. There was silence until I said, "It's too late, isn't it?"

"Sorry," Suki said, and she did sound kind of sorry. "I think I might have maybe already told her."

Oh, no! Now Zinny knew that I knew, and she probably knew that I knew that she knew—so I couldn't pretend that I didn't know! How would I act around her?

"Honesty is the best policy," Suki said. "Right?"

"Hmmmm," I said, not at all sure that it was right.

I said good-bye, hung up, put The Boys back in their cage, and started worrying for real.

The next day was a Sunday, so I went with my mom to the shelter. A mother possum, nursing her nine babies, had fallen off a roof and died, but all the babies, still suckling away, had lived. Someone found that sad group in their yard and brought them in. The mom was buried before I got there.

Rita was in the office with the box of babies. We each got a tiny bottle of formula and we sat together feeding one baby possum after another. I felt so warm and nice feeding them that I forgot that Rita was not a *real* girl. I forgot that you can't trust a puppet. I just opened my mouth and the whole raccoon story gushed out.

"She drowned it?" Rita asked. "This is a *friend* of yours? Someone you *like*?"

I was instantly sorry I'd said anything. "My friend didn't do it," I said, "her mom did."

"Did you tell your parents?" Rita asked.

"No."

"Well, you should. You should tell them right now."

"I'm not going to," I said, "and you have to promise that you won't either."

"I will promise no such thing!" huffed Rita in her Rita-the-Great voice. "I don't even think it's legal, what she did."

"Rita, please." Now I was really begging. "It would make everything entirely horrid if you told. Please don't tell. *Please?*"

Rita just looked at me like I was the stupidest, most pathetic thing on legs.

I banged out the door and ran down the hill to where the parrots were screeching. The giant macaw, Phil, came to the edge of his aviary to see if I had brought any snacks, but I could hardly even see him. "Breathe in, breathe out," I told myself, feeling like I was going to faint.

Was Rita going to tell my folks what I'd told her? Had I told Rita Zinny's name, or did I just say "my friend"? Rita wouldn't have to be a rocket scientist to figure out it was Zinny, though, even if I didn't say her name. It's not like I had *that* many friends, and I'd told Rita about Zinny before, and how her family didn't like animals.

I don't know how much time passed, but eventually I noticed my stomach was feeling funny. I thought maybe I was hungry, so I went back up to the office. Eli was wallowing in the dirt, sticking raven feathers into anthills. Rita was inside the office reading a book with Slinky, the lame ferret, asleep on her lap. She glanced up when I came in and gave me a look that was supposed to mean something—but I didn't know what.

My mom was in surgery. I got my lunch and crept off to eat it under the olive tree near the goats' pen.

My tuna sandwich felt bad going down, and every time I burped, it tasted like tuna again. In the car on the way home I felt worse.

"Mom?" I said. "I don't feel good."

"Open the window, get some air," she said, but before I could do so, I threw up all over the seat, all over the car door, and all over myself.

My mom tried to be a good sport, but I could tell she was grossed out. We were miles from nowhere and had to ride with the puke smell for ages before we got to a Taco Bell. My mom made me go into the women's room, past all the people eating, to clean myself up. She got a million napkins and went to work on her car upholstery. Still, it stank all the way home.

After my bath I called Zinny. "It's Ava," I said.

"Hey!" she said. She said it in a perfectly friendly, normal way.

"Hey, yourself," I said. "I threw up in my mom's car. All over everything!"

"*Gross!*" she shrieked, and we giggled together.

"Guess I won't be in school tomorrow," I said.

"You lucky lou," Zinny snorted. "I wish I could barf my way out of tomorrow's math test." I'd forgotten all about the test. We talked a while longer until my mom made me hang up. And that was that. Things seemed totally normal.

I wondered if maybe being the daughter of two vets made me overly sensitive about animals. Rita's opinion didn't count either, because number one, she was a puppet, and number two, she had animal fanatic parents too. Maybe to the rest of the world a raccoon's death was no big deal. After all, people set rat and mouse traps all the time. People hunt for fun and hang deer heads on their walls, they kill minks for coats and cart old horses off to the glue factory—and no one bats an eye.

So was it *all* terrible, or was *none* of it terrible? Could things be just a little terrible? The more confused I felt, the more I wondered if maybe I wasn't such a great judge of right and wrong.

I realized that if it was up to me, no animals would ever be killed for anything. But I also knew that was unreasonable. Plus it wasn't absolutely true, because I ate cheeseburgers and tuna fish.

Although after that afternoon, I didn't plan on eating tuna for a mighty long time, if ever again.

My brain got so tired of twisting that it finally, finally fell asleep and left me in peace—except for a few nightmares.

The next day I hung around the house feeling a little wobbly about food, but otherwise fine. My mom stayed home from the clinic and we looked through the drawer of old photos that she always says she's going to put in an album.

"Mom," I asked, "how do you feel about killing animals?"

"You mean how do I feel when I have to put an animal down?"

I *didn't* mean that—but since she asked, I said, "Yes."

"Well, it's never easy. Even when I know it's a real mercy killing, that the animal is suffering terribly—and I'm sure there is nothing else I can do to ease its pain . . . there's always a teeny voice in me that says miracles do happen. Every now and then an animal mysteriously gets better. . . ."

I thought about that. Thought of my mom and dad giving lethal injections to dogs and cats. Mrs. Weston had "put down" one raccoon. I'd never really thought about it before, but my own animal-lover parents had probably killed hundreds of animals between them.

"What's much worse, infinitely worse," Mom said in a quieter voice, "is when I have to destroy a healthy animal just because its owners want me to . . . because it soiled their rugs or dug up their garden."

"Can't you say no?"

"Sometimes Daddy and I lie," she whispered, smiling at me. "Sometimes we say we'll do it, but when the owners leave, we try to adopt the pet out instead."

"But other times you go ahead and give the shot?"

My mom nodded. "For better or worse, humans rule the world," she said. "Sometimes wisely, sometimes not. And there are so many, many unwanted pets, more every day, every hour. . . ." Then she clapped her hands and said, "Well, that's enough of that. Want to play cards?"

Later I watched my lizard, Rock, scrape against a branch in his tank, trying to shed. He pulled and peeled his loose skin with his mouth. I was nearly hypnotized watching him when the phone rang right next to me, making me jump.

I picked it up and said, "Hello."

Zinny said, "Hey."

"Hey, yourself." Zinny was home after school, calling to tell me about the math test and Crystal's new, really short haircut. "And guess what?" Zinny said. "Mr. Draper asked Melinda to just mouth the words at the Spring Program, or sing *very* softly!"

"Zinny! That's a riot!" I squealed. "Was she horribly embarrassed?"

"Mortified!"

While we were laughing, Rock slid out of his last bits of old skin. He was shiny new and beautifully bright. Somehow that made me feel brave.

"Zinny," I said, "about that . . . you know."

"Alien abductor?" Zinny asked quietly.

"Yeah," I said. Then I didn't know what else to say. There was nothing but breathing on both ends of the phone for a while, until I asked, "Were you there?"

"No."

"Good," I said. "Well, anyway . . ."

And Zinny said, "I know." There was more silence. "So, I'll see you in the morning?"

I said, "Yeah." Then we both said good-bye and hung up.

The next morning Zinny and I met in front of my house and walked all the way to school backward. Neither of us tripped. The school day was okay too. And just like when our dads had fought about Honey Bunny and the petunias, neither Zinny nor I mentioned the alien abductor murder at all.

At our rehearsal for the Spring Program, Mr. Draper played the piano for our warm-ups. Then he got out his banjo and said, "Let's take a stab at 'Sweet Betsy from Pike.'" My stomach got fluttery. "This song is about getting to California during the gold rush days," he explained. "It wasn't easy. But this brave gal and her slightly less brave sweetheart made it here. Some of your ancestors probably got here the same way. Are you ready, Ava?"

Mr. Draper played a riff on his banjo and nodded at me to jump in. I did. " 'Did you ever hear of sweet Betsy from Pike, who crossed the wide prairie with her lover Ike? With two yoke of cattle and one spotted hog, a tall Shanghai rooster and an old yaller dog.' "

Mr. Draper nodded to the rest of the class and they chimed in, " 'Sing too ra li, oo ra li, oo ra li ay.' "

We were up in Zinny's room after school, telling horror stories. Zinny's stories were about her old, creaky house back in Chicago. It was haunted by a family of ghosts who all died miserable, gruesome deaths long ago. My stories were about the ax-murderer drummer who lived downstairs in our old apartment building. He banged on his drums to cover the ghastly screams of his victims. We were scaring ourselves and each other pretty good. I had chills running down my neck. Then we were startled by a hammering on the front door.

Mrs. Weston had just run out to the store, so we were alone. We flew downstairs and Zinny called through the closed door, "We aren't here," which made us giggle. She looked through the peephole at the man on the front porch. I looked out the window and saw a second man walk across the lawn and peer over the gate into the backyard.

"*Zinny!* There are two of them! We're surrounded!"

We both started screaming. Every horror movie I'd ever seen ran straight through my head.

"Go away!" Zinny shrieked. "We're calling the police!" She told me to call 911. I was halfway to the phone when Mrs. Weston's station wagon pulled up in the driveway. I heard the garage door open and thought, Oh, no! What if they follow her in and kill all three of us?

Then Mrs. Weston came in the garage door to the kitchen and called out a cheery, "Hello?"

I heard the tick-tick of her high heels on the floor as she walked past Zinny to the front door and opened it. She smiled at the man there and, calm as can be, said, "Yes? May I help you?"

The man said, "We're from Animal Protection, ma'am. We've received a report of animal cruelty here and would like to inspect the premises."

I looked at Zinny. She looked at me. Her mom stared at the man and asked, "What report? Cruelty to what animal?"

The look in Zinny's eyes turned ice-cold, colder than I'd thought possible. She grabbed my arm hard—and it hurt. She brought her frozen face close to mine and snarled, "Ava, what have you done?"

"Me? I haven't done anything!" I said. "Really, Zinny. I haven't done *anything*."

"Sure," she spat, shoving me toward the door. "Get out of here." When I didn't budge, she repeated, louder, *"Get out, Ava!"*

"But, but . . ." I sputtered, but she'd turned her back on me. I went out the door and looked up at the man on the porch. I jumped. "Mike?" It was Mike from the shelter. He brought in animals all the time. He'd brought in Honey. I could feel Zinny and her mother looking at us.

Mike looked at me and said, "Ava?"

I moved down to the front walk and stood there, probably with my mouth hanging open.

I guess Zinny's mom had given Mike and the other man permission to search the yard, because they were moving all over it.

I backed off farther, not knowing what to do. What would Mike find—the trap? Did Zinny's mom throw the dead raccoon in the garbage or bury it or what?

I stood in prickly hot panic, thinking, I didn't do this, did I? Did Rita tell her dad, and her dad tell my dad, and my dad tell Mike?

Eventually Mike went back to the front porch and I could see him talking to Mrs. Weston. Then he and the other guy got in their truck and left. At least they didn't take Zinny's mom with them!

I felt sorry for Zinny and sorry for me that I was being blamed. And sorry that I had told Rita about the raccoon, and sorry that I knew Mike.

Every cell in my body wanted to go knock on Zinny's door and tell her that I was sorry, sorry,

sorry. Except for the one little itty-bitty part of my heart that said you can't just kill an innocent raccoon and get away with it.

The garage door opened, and Zinny's mom's station wagon backed down the driveway. Were they going to the police station? As the car passed me, Zinny rolled down her window and yelled, "Proud of yourself, Ava?"

To say that I felt sick is too simple. To say that I was totally ill and diseased in every inch of my bones and drop of blood and bit of flesh is not enough. How can I tell you how ashamed and hurt and guilty and innocent and confused and sorry I was?

However miserable I was, it must have shown, because as soon as I walked in the door of my house, my mom dropped the bag of frozen peas she was holding and rushed toward me, saying, "What is it? What happened?"

She hugged me tight. It was then that I realized my teeth were chattering. My mom asked louder, "What happened? Are you hurt?" Her eyes searched my face. "It'll be okay, Ava," she said. "Just tell me. . . ." But I could only cry.

Mom inched us over to a chair. She held me on her lap like I was a little girl and she rocked me, cooing in the same voice she used on frightened animals at the clinic.

My mom let me cry a while, then said, "Ava, it's time to tell me what happened. Whatever it is, it's time to tell."

Did she really not know? Could my dad have reported Mrs. Weston and not told Mom about it? It didn't seem likely. My parents talk about everything—so much so that it's usually hard for me to get a word in edgewise.

"Ava, did anyone do anything to hurt you? Did anyone touch you?"

"No, no! It's nothing like that." For a second I felt giddy with relief. My parents didn't turn in Mrs. Weston! I didn't do it! It really wasn't my fault!

"Then what *is* it? You have to tell me. Now."

"Well . . ." I thought about how to explain without telling Mom about the raccoon. "It's just that Zinny's mom might be in a lot of trouble for doing something, and Zinny thinks I'm the one that told on her, and so Zinny hates me and I don't blame her, except that I didn't tell, really."

"If Mrs. Weston did something that bad then it's her fault she got in trouble, not the person who told on her."

"Well, it's not her fault that she got caught."

"We're not supposed to do things that we don't want to be caught doing," my mom said. "I think you better tell me what she did."

"I can't. I don't want you to hate her. *I* kind of hate her, but Zinny is my best friend, at least she was . . ."

"Did Mrs. Weston do anything that endangered you in any way?"

"No."

"Then why does Zinny think you're the one who told on her mother?"

I took a deep breath. I had to tell my mom something. If not the whole truth, at least part of it. "She didn't do anything to me," I said. "She did something to, um, to endanger an animal. A wild animal. And they think I told on her because they know I'm an animal lover and you and Dad are vets. Please, Mom, I don't want to tell you any more than that."

My mom started to protest. I know she wanted all the details, but then she stopped herself. "If you're absolutely positive that no one did anything at all to hurt you in any way"—her eyes drilled into mine—"then I'll try to respect your privacy."

"Thanks," I said, cuddling deeper into her lap.

"But when you are ready to talk about it, you know I'm ready to listen," she added.

"I know."

The relief didn't last long. All I had to do was remember that icicle look on Zinny's face, and the way she practically spat at me to get out of her house, and my guts would shrivel up inside me.

Then I realized that if it really, really wasn't Rita who told on Mrs. Weston, then it had to have been Suki's mom.

After all, it was Suki who told me about the murder, and *her* mom had told her. I had to talk to Suki! She was the only one who could explain to Zinny and clear my name.

I noticed that my fingers were shaking when I dialed Suki's number. When her mom answered, I wanted so badly to ask her if she had called Animal Protection, but my mouth wouldn't do it. Instead, I asked if Suki was home. Her mom put the phone down for a long time. Then she came back and said Suki was busy and would call me back.

I waited—no Suki. I called again, but when Suki's mom answered a second time, I hung up.

We hadn't even had dinner yet, but I crawled into bed. I didn't read, just pulled the blankets up high and stared at the ceiling. After a while my mom came in with a toasted bagel and a glass of juice on a tray.

I took a bite of bagel. "Mom?"

"Yes, sweetie."

"I know this sounds dumb, but which is more important, animals or people?"

"It doesn't sound dumb at all. I guess, since you and Dad are the most important things in the world to me, and you are people—I think people are more important."

"I mean, not just us, but for the world."

"Well, that's a hard question. Even grown-ups don't agree. Remember when those animal rights activists blew up a research lab because people performed experiments on animals there? And the explosion killed a student who was working late? Those protesters thought animals were more important than people."

"Wow."

"People are always arguing about our place in the universe—human rights as opposed to animal rights. It is not a simple problem at all. If you were sick and there was a new drug that might cure you, I would need to know that that drug had been thoroughly tested on living things. I wouldn't want *you* to be the experiment. But do I want innocent animals to be pumped full of experimental drugs that make them suffer?" Mom shrugged helplessly. "I don't know. There's no answer."

And then my mom did something she hasn't done for years. She turned off the light and lay down in bed next to me till I fell asleep.

In the morning I woke up—not to the alarm clock, but to the sound of construction across the street. The clock read 10:15.

I jumped out of bed and pulled on some clothes. "Hey!" I called out. "I gotta get to school!"

My dad came into the room.

"You stayed home from work?" I asked.

He shrugged as if staying home was no big deal. "You slept through the alarm and Mommy tried to wake you twice. We thought maybe you were still sick."

"I'm fine, Dad," I said, "and I've *really* got to get to school."

My dad looked doubtful but agreed to drive me. He was probably glad to get back to the clinic, imagining the waiting room mobbed with cats, dogs, and their cranky owners. And I was anxious to see Suki, sure that I'd be able to fix things up the second I got a chance to talk to her. She would tell Zinny that the whole thing had nothing to do with me. Zinny would say she was sorry she'd blamed me. I'd say, "That's okay," and it *would* be okay.

So I was shocked when I charged into my classroom and saw Suki's desk empty. I looked around— no Suki. And there was Zinny, looking anywhere but at me. I gave Mrs. Hicks the tardy excuse from my dad and sat down.

"Well, Ava," Mrs. Hicks said, "you timed your entrance just right. I was about to explain our spring social studies project. We are going to break up into groups of three. Each group will select a country democratically. That means you'll vote among yourselves. . . ."

As my teacher droned on about how this was a "long-term" project, I tried to catch Zinny's eye, but she wouldn't let me. Then everyone got up and started swarming around. I hadn't been listening, but Mrs. Hicks must have told us to form our groups. In the less than two seconds it took me to get up, Zinny had two partners selected—neither of them me.

I looked around and saw that Melinda, my ex-tormentor, was the last one alone. Neither of us budged. Mrs. Hicks came over to me and pointed out Melinda, as if I couldn't see her. I had no choice but to go sit next to her. Just how much worse could things get?

"I suppose you want to do some country like Rwanda," Melinda said.

"Not particularly, why?" I asked, walking right into it.

"Isn't that where gorillas come from?" Melinda asked.

Oh. That's how much worse things could get. Melinda was still willing to resurrect the gorilla taunt.

I didn't have a good comeback, or even a so-so comeback. I couldn't help looking over at Zinny's group: Zinny, Jason—the one Zinny had a crush on—and Crystal. Did Crystal hate me too?

Melinda and I were supposed to be working on the social studies project, but my brain was like scrambled eggs. We grudgingly made plans to meet at my house after school. We had no intention of walking home from school together.

I don't know who I felt worse for right then, me or Zinny. My best friend hated me and I was stuck doing a project with Melinda. But poor Zinny— imagine how it felt to have your mom in trouble with the police. A criminal! That meant lawyers, a judge, a courtroom . . . *Yech!*

Later, at the Spring Program rehearsal, I started to sing "Sweet Betsy," but my throat was so tight and dry that my voice came out in a frog's croak. Kids snickered. I didn't look to see if Zinny was one of the snickerers.

After that long, ugly school day, I saw Zinny leave with Crystal. I knew she was going to Crystal's house because they turned left at the corner. I walked home alone, feeling like Sweet Betsy crossing the desert, only I didn't have an Ike. One verse kept running through my mind: "That alkali desert was burning and bare, and Ike cried in fear, 'We are lost, I declare. My dear old Pike County, I'll come back to you.' Said Betsy, 'You'll go by yourself if you do.'"

But by the time I got home, I felt my mood changing. Bit by bit I felt less sad and more angry. I liked *mad* a lot more than *sad*. Neither of my parents were home yet, so I took Ralph out for his walk. Usually it's hard to stay mad around Ralph, but this time it was easy. "I'm totally sick of being such a wimp!" I told him, and he barked.

I stomped back into the house and called Suki. No answer. I called Crystal's house and she picked up on the first ring. "Crystal, let me talk to Zinny," I said, ready to really let her have it.

"Just a second, *Ava*," Crystal said. I heard whispering and giggling. Then Crystal said, "Zinny's not here." I slammed down the receiver and went from mad to furious.

Who needed a friend like Zinnia Weston? Who needed a friend who was so ready to think the worst of me? Who needed any of them? Who needed to be treated like dirt? *Not me.*

Ralph started barking his head off when the doorbell rang. There was Melinda—I'd forgotten she was coming.

"I can't stay," Melinda said, instead of "hello." "I've gotta do some stuff." She walked in the door and sniffed. "It stinks in here. Isn't that dog house-broken?"

She went over to the couch and was about to sit down but didn't. I looked at the couch and saw why. It was Ralph's favorite spot, and Melinda probably didn't want dog hair on her black jeans.

I saw her glance around the living room at the coffee cups and newspapers, the heap of half-folded laundry, the feathers and bird seed scattered on the floor around the birdcage. . . .

"So we'll have to talk about the social studies thing later or something," Melinda said, heading out the door, which I still held open. "Ta-ta, Go-ril-la!" and she was gone.

Had I said a single word?

Does it stink in here? I wondered. Is that why Zinny always ran around opening the windows?

After my heart slowed down, I nearly started cleaning up the living room. I was halfway to the closet where I suspected the vacuum cleaner was kept when I changed my mind.

"If Sweet Betsy from Pike could cross the wild prairie," I said out loud, "I should at least be able to stand up to one puny Melinda." Ralph looked up at me.

I got Melinda's phone number and left a message on her machine saying that, yes, I did want to do our project on Rwanda, where gorillas come from. I also said I would dress in a gorilla suit for the oral part of the presentation and talk about life in Rwanda from the gorilla's point of view.

Then I looked up the number for Animal Control and called them. I told the woman who answered the phone that I was doing a paper for class and asked her what they did to people who killed animals in a mean way.

"The penalty depends on the judge," she said. "It could be anywhere from nothing to a year in prison or ten thousand dollars."

I asked what proof they needed, and she said they had to either see the animal itself or have a witness willing to testify.

"Does 'willing to testify' mean that the killer will find out who tattled on them? Or can you be a witness in secret?"

"They have to come forth," the woman said,

which I guessed meant they couldn't be sneaky about it. That also meant that if Mike didn't find the raccoon's body, then whoever reported Mrs. Weston would have to either come forth, proving that they weren't me—or not come forth, and Zinny would never know it wasn't me.

I didn't want Mrs. Weston to go to jail, but I wanted Zinny to find out it wasn't me. Then I wanted her to feel wretchedly ashamed that she'd blamed me. I wanted her to grovel and beg me to forgive her. And then I wanted to say, "No."

She'd tell me how she missed me and how horribly guilty and lonely she felt, how she couldn't eat or sleep—and I'd just shrug and say, "Oh, well." Or I'd smile sweetly and say, "You'll get over it." Or I wouldn't be at all sweet when I said, "I wouldn't be your friend again for anything. You are scum, Zinnia Victoria Weston—septic, germ-infested, chemically polluted pond scum."

I guess I'd spaced out on the phone because the Animal Protection lady was saying, "Hello? Hello?"

"What if the witness didn't see it happen, just heard about it?" I asked her.

"That depends who they heard it from," she said, "the person who committed the act or a third person. Third person is hearsay, inadmissible evidence. No judge would rule on hearsay."

Hearsay. I felt my neck prickle. I had judged Zinny's mom on hearsay. I didn't see anyone drown a raccoon. In fact, I never even saw the raccoon. All I saw was a trap in the Westons' backyard. The rest was gossip. Maybe no more than neighbors flapping their lips. I was no better than Zinny, the septic pond scum.

I didn't even know if Suki's mom had watched Mrs. Weston drown the raccoon or if Mrs. Weston just told her about it. And why would she tell anyone that? I pictured their conversation:

Mrs. Weston: "Hi, what's new?"

Suki's mom: "Nothing much. How about you?"

Mrs. Weston: "Well, I had my nails done, then I drowned a raccoon in my garbage can with the garden hose. Now I'm thinking about making tuna noodle casserole for dinner."

I know grown-ups are strange, but can they be *that* strange?

"Are you still there?" came the Animal Protection woman's voice. I thanked her and hung up.

I went out in the backyard and noticed right away that Honey Bunny was acting bizarre. She was zooming around way faster than I'd ever seen her go before. She yanked up a mouthful of grass, then dove into the bushes. I heard her thrash around down there, then out she popped. She frantically grabbed more grass and made another dive. When she scrambled back out, she started tearing the fur out of her chest with her teeth!

I watched all this and felt fear twist my gut. I ran

inside to call the clinic. It rang forever, then, "Fins, Fangs, Feathers, and Fur," said my parents' receptionist.

"Doreen? It's Ava. Quick, get my dad. Honey Bunny has been poisoned!"

My dad came on the line with his professional voice. "What are her symptoms?" he asked.

My words jumbled over each other. Then I heard my dad laugh! "Ava, Ava, calm down. Honey isn't dying, she's pregnant!"

"What?"

"She's making a burrow under the bush," he said.

"Pulling out her own fur?" I asked, wondering if he'd really heard me.

"To make a nice soft nest of grass and fur for her babies." He chuckled again and said, "You're going to be a grandmother!"

I let that sink into my brain. Baby bunnies. I love baby bunnies!

"Mom should be home any second," my dad said. "We got tied up in surgery this afternoon. Have her check Honey out when she gets there, to see how far along she is."

I went out to give Honey a pretzel, but she was so busy I could hardly get her attention. When she did dart up to nab her snack, I looked at her more closely. She didn't look pregnant, at least not hugely pregnant like women at the mall looked sometimes, but she didn't look poisoned either.

I smiled. Not only had I been sure Honey had been poisoned, but I was also ready to believe that I knew exactly who had done it and why. I was glad to be wrong.

To celebrate Honey's news, I set the table while my mom made salad and my dad opened a can of food for Ralph. My mom was not as thrilled about it as me and Dad were, though.

Mom said, "We should have spayed Honey Bunny when we first got her. We'll do it for sure after this litter. She could have half a dozen babies at once, you know."

"Wow!"

"And then, in no time, those babies can start having babies. And Honey can get pregnant with another litter almost as soon as she's done nursing this batch."

I could picture our backyard completely full of miniature Honey Bunnies, hopping every which way, their soft noses twitching.

"Don't laugh, Ava, it's serious," she said. "We have to find homes for every one of those babies or they'll overrun the neighborhood." But she was smiling.

"Your friend Zinny's father will love that!" my dad said. "There won't be a petunia for miles."

I stopped laughing. In a flash I saw all my sweet babies in traps, Mrs. Weston trotting out her garden hose. I saw rabbit-fur throw pillows on the Westons' couch, and a "lucky" rabbit's foot dangling from each of their keychains.

Dinner was ready and we all sat down. My dad raised his water glass and said, "I propose a toast to Honey Bunny and her babies. May they live long and multiply!"

I raised my glass to clink with his and Mom's, but my hand was shaking so badly that I spilled water all over the table.

Because Suki had been absent when we divided into groups for the social studies project, and since Melinda and I had only two in our group, Mrs. Hicks led Suki over to us the next day. Suki walked slowly, head down, as if she were marching to the guillotine.

I waited to see if she would bring up the subject of the raccoon, but she didn't say anything at all. She just plucked at her sweatshirt with nervous, skinny fingers.

Zinny ignored me smoothly, as if I wasn't there, but Suki wasn't acting nearly as cool about it. She plucked and suffered. I almost felt bad for her, but not quite.

When I couldn't stand it anymore, I said, "Suki, we have to talk about—"

But she cut me off and in a timid little squeak said, "Let's just talk about geography, okay?"

"Not okay," I said.

"I'm not going to talk about it," Suki whispered, her face blushing redder and redder.

Melinda looked from Suki to me. "What's this, a gorilla fight?" she sneered. Neither of us answered her.

"Suki," I began, but she interrupted me again.

"I am not talking about it!" Her face was now so incredibly red, I wondered if her head would pop. Maybe it would explode all over Melinda.

There was a big three-way silence. Then I told them that we should divide the project up into parts and work separately. I told them I was going to do a gorilla's perspective on Rwanda and they could do whatever they wanted. I could not care less.

"You weren't kidding?" Melinda said. "The gorilla suit and all?"

"It's supposed to be a group project," Suki said, her fingers plucking wildly. "We'll get in trouble."

"Tough," I said, and that was that.

I bolted out of school the second the bell rang. I didn't want to run into Zinny and Crystal and Suki. I didn't want to know who was going to whose house. And I especially didn't want to find myself trailing along behind Zinny, with her pretending I wasn't there. I took a roundabout way home, passing blocks and blocks of identical houses. I wished we still lived in our old apartment—drummer and all. I wished I still went to my old school with kids who liked me and had known me since kindergarten. I'd meant to keep in touch with those kids. I decided I'd call up Rachel, my old best friend, when I got home. I hadn't done that in a while.

Suddenly Ralph bounded up to me. I heard my dad whistle for him, but Ralph ignored him and jumped up to give me a lick. My dad came around the corner and waved.

We started walking home together. "Why did we move here?" I asked him. "It's a stupid place."

"Places can't be stupid," Dad said. "And anyway, I think it's sort of interesting."

"Interesting? It all looks the same!"

Dad laughed. "The other day I was walking Ralph and I went home to the wrong house. I went all the way in the door and stood around in the front hall, looking at an unfamiliar painting hanging over an unfamiliar chair. I wondered if I'd lost my mind. I call that an interesting experience."

"You didn't really!" I said.

"I did! A woman poked her head out of the kitchen and screamed!"

"No!"

"Ralph was outside, barking up a storm, trying to warn me, but I thought he just didn't want to come home."

I laughed, but then I remembered how awful my life was. "I hate it here," I said. "The people are stupid. Stupid and mean."

"People are people everywhere you go, Ava. You might as well get used to us."

When we got home, I called Rachel. I still remembered her number by heart. She was so happy to hear from me that I almost cried. But then, when she started telling me about the other kids at school, it all sounded so fun and so familiar that I *really* almost cried.

"And how is your new school?" Rachel asked.

I wanted to tell her that I was lonely. Wanted to tell her about Zinny pretending I was invisible and Melinda calling me Gorilla, and about Suki and Crystal turning against me. I wanted to say that I missed her so badly that I just wanted to move back *home*. . . .

But I said, "It's great. The kids are really nice. And I got a big solo in the Spring Program."

"That's neat," Rachel said. "I'm so glad you called, Ava. We all miss you. But I've gotta go. Jenny and my mom are waiting in the car. We're going to be late for gymnastics."

"Tell Jenny I said hi," I said.

"I will."

"Ava thinks we moved to the wrong neighborhood," Dad said to Mom at dinner.

"She and Zinny are having problems," Mom said, speaking as if I wasn't there.

"No surprise there," Dad said. "That Zinny comes from one strange family. Her father in particular. Remember the time he came over here with Honey—"

"We all remember, dear," my mom interrupted.

I poked at my chicken pot pie, knowing my mom was making "shut up" faces at my dad across the table.

"All I'm saying is that kid *has* to be nuts having a father like that." Then he looked at me and said, "Why don't you get some friends with normal parents?"

"You mean like mine?" I asked in the sweetest voice I could come up with.

"Everybody just eat," Mom said.

Whenever I could get one of my parents out the door in time, I had them drive me to school. And when I walked home, I took a different route each afternoon. One day I walked past a construction site, with huge bulldozers and cranes frozen in position around a half-built house. It looked as if they were holding very, very still so I wouldn't notice them. As if I'd taken them by surprise and caught them feeding on that newly killed house. They didn't have time to take cover behind those scraggly new trees, so they just held their breath and hoped I wouldn't spot them. I knew that as soon as I passed, they'd go back to devouring that house. It was a grim scene.

I remembered Zinny saying she and I were Eve and Eve. Now it was just me, first human girl, friendless, in the land of the dinosaurs. I wondered if this was what my dad meant by the subdivision being "interesting."

Another afternoon, when I was almost two blocks from home, I saw Honey Bunny nibbling flowers on some stranger's front lawn. She didn't seem to recognize me until I began singing "Little Bunny Foo-Foo." Then she hopped up to search my hands for treats. I picked her up and carried her all the rest of the way home, singing softly into her fur.

When my dad and I got to the shelter that Sunday, I couldn't bear to watch Rita arranging papers at the desk, getting her pens all lined up neatly— and just generally being a fussy old hen. I grabbed the bucket of carrots, the white paper cups, and the knife, and headed down to the petting zoo. I knew I was being rude, but the thought that I was back to having only Rita the puppet as my friend seemed more pathetic than having no friends at all.

I was cutting up carrots to sell to the tourists. They liked to feed the goats and pigs. I could see the parking lot from where I sat. I didn't realize what I was watching for until the Animal Protection truck pulled up. I squinted at the man who got out. He wasn't Mike.

This time it wasn't Mike, but one of these days it would be, and what would he tell my dad? I knew that Zinny already hated me, and probably things couldn't really get much worse. But the thought of my parents hearing about the raccoon drowning from Mike gave me the shivers. Mostly I was afraid that if Mike saw me, he'd ask me about that day at the Westons', and I'd either have to tell him what I knew or lie to him. Both those choices were creepy. I figured I just had to hide from him forever.

When my dad and I were safely on our way home, I asked him if he'd seen Mike lately.

"Mike?"

"You know, *Mike.* Animal Protection Mike."

"All those uniforms look the same to me" was my dad's reply.

———

I started going to the library after school. I was glad to have someplace to go besides straight home. I was also getting really interested in reading about gorillas. They are, it turns out, incredibly cool.

Melinda thought it was such a huge insult to call me Gorilla, but the more I learned about them, the more I thought being a gorilla would be just fine. I'd travel in a big crowd of females, led by one big male called a silverback. He'd lead us to the good food and he'd protect us from our enemies, and all day we'd just play and eat and walk around the jungle together. One of the books said that when two gorillas fight over a piece of food or something, the silverback just stares at them or grunts a couple times and the fight is over. Everything is instantly peaceful and friendly again, and everyone gets along.

I sat at a library table in the corner thinking that if one gorilla didn't have a lot of fur, the others wouldn't call her *human* just to make her feel bad. And they wouldn't gang up on her, and all suddenly decide to stop talking to her.

Once I went up to the librarian to ask her if she had any more books on Koko, the gorilla who talked in sign language. When I opened my mouth to speak, I realized that those were the first words

I'd said since saying good-bye to my mom that morning!

I would sing at the Spring Program rehearsals, and if Mrs. Hicks called on me, I'd answer questions in class. But besides that, whole school days passed without me speaking to a soul.

I felt like I was alone in a foreign country. When we went to France one summer, it had felt so strange not to be able to read any of the billboards or store names or menus or labels. The TV was all in French and the newspapers too. It was a little scary, everyone talking so fast and making no sense at all.

In this case I had no way of finding out what was happening with Mrs. Weston. I guessed that if Zinny was still blaming me, then Suki's mom must not have "come forth" to testify. But I had no news and no way to get news. It was France all over again, except in France I'd had my parents with me, and now I was all alone.

I was in the library at my usual corner table, reading about how endangered gorillas were. It was so horribly sad that I felt guilty being human. After all, it was my species that was killing them off. These big, gentle animals were just minding their own business and along we came to hunt them down. The book said that for every gorilla that reaches the zoo, at least two die on the way. But it's really deforestation that's wiping them out, by taking away their food and their home.

That's a typical example of the kind of thing our parents' parents, and I guess even our own parents, did. First they had a jolly time polluting all the water and air. Then they said "oops" and left us to clean up their mess. And now that they've hacked down miles of forest and killed off all kinds of animals, we are left to come up with some way to save the last few.

But I wondered if we were going to be any more careful and kind to the earth than other generations had been. I doubted that the Melindas and Zinnys of the world were going to take the extinction of the gorillas very seriously.

The stuff I was reading was so interesting that I forgot about everything else until I felt someone beside me. I looked up. There was Crystal, clutching her books to her chest.

"Hi, Ava," she said.

"Hi," I answered. "I didn't know you were still talking to me."

Crystal looked down at her shoes. "Sure, of course I'm talking to you, I mean . . . "

"You mean because Zinny's not here to see you," I said, very calmly, considering.

Crystal looked at her shoes some more. "What's going on with you and Zinny?" she asked.

"Ask her," I said, pretending to return to my gorilla book.

"I did ask her."

"And?"

"She won't say," said Crystal. "Suki says it's about that raccoon thing. You're mad at Zinny because of what her mother did."

I thought about that. At least Zinny wasn't saying mean things about me behind my back. Maybe she just didn't want to talk about what her mom did. After all, she couldn't talk about *me* without telling everyone that her mom got in trouble. And Suki couldn't say much because she knew her mom was the one who told on Mrs. Weston, and she didn't want anyone to know.

Crystal's big brother came up. "Come on, Crys, we gotta go."

Crystal kept looking at the floor.

"Now!" said her brother.

Crystal said, "Bye," and followed her brother out.

Was that "bye" for now or "bye" forever? I tried to crawl back into the jungle world of the gorillas, but the words wouldn't lie flat on the page. I checked out a few gorilla books and went out front to wait for my mom.

Neither Crystal nor Suki had been my friends before Zinny came along. Certainly neither of them had dared to like me when Melinda was

boss. And here we were back where we started—
Suki and Crystal scared to be my friends because
someone else didn't like me. And Crystal wasn't
even sure why!

As I paced back and forth in front of the library,
I wondered what I would have done if Zinny had
suddenly decided to hate Suki or Crystal. Would I
have had the guts to still be friends with them? I'd
like to think I would. If I were perfect, I would. But
if Zinny had wanted me to choose between her
and them . . .

Nothing is easy. At least not for me.

Each day lurched along like it had square wheels.
The only school hours that were bearable were the
rehearsals for the Spring Program. Even if not one
kid there was my friend, it still felt good to hear all
our voices together, harmonizing. Even the times
we didn't get around to "Sweet Betsy," the singing
felt right.

If it wasn't for rehearsals at school and my pets
at home, I would have gone totally and completely
nuts. I taught Hug, my lovebird, to fly right to me
and take a Cheerio from between my lips. I tried
to teach Kiss too, but she wasn't interested. I
brushed and brushed Ralph's fur. I rearranged
Shelly and Michelle's mini-beach-in-a-tub to make
their life more interesting. I gave Honey extra
treats. I even set up a maze to race The Boys. I
practiced my solo and read about gorillas.

My parents were glad that I was interested in gorillas. I think they secretly hoped I'd be a vet someday. Sometimes the rescued exotic animals at the shelter are placed at the zoo in town, so my folks know a bunch of people there. My mom asked me if I'd like to meet the zoo's primate keeper.

"Sure," I said.

So one Sunday instead of going to the shelter with my dad, I went into town to the zoo with my mom. If I hadn't been totally in love with gorillas before that, I sure would have been afterward. The babies were adorable, and their moms were so sweet and patient with them. The males swished tree branches in the air and chased each other around. Then they sat down and very seriously picked their noses, looking right at us.

My mom and I split an order of animal-shaped french fries and watched the gorillas watch the humans, until it was time to meet Mom's friend George. He shook my hand and asked me how I got interested in gorillas. I didn't think the Melinda story would sound right, so I just mumbled something about liking animals.

Then George led us "backstage." He showed us the gorillas' night quarters, which were inside and looked like jail cells. We watched him prepare their food. He told me that gorillas were vegetarians, but I already knew that. He also told me that the zoo's breeding program was trying to increase the gorilla population—to pull them back from the brink of extinction and release them in the wild again someday. I didn't tell him that I knew how many gorillas died on the way to zoos. It wasn't his fault.

Then a gorilla lumbered through the door into his night cage. He was pretty scary-looking. George didn't let us get too close, but my mom and I were near enough to see how really huge he was.

"This is Buddy," George said. "He's five years old and weighs four hundred pounds, more or less." Mom and I watched George hold a glass of milk to Buddy's lips. "Each of them drinks a glass of milk a day," George said. Buddy didn't pay any attention to us. He drank his milk and paced around the cage a couple times, then he swung back outside.

My mom looked at me and laughed. "Your eyes are as big as moons!" she said.

On the way home she asked me if I thought I'd like a job like George's, now that I was so interested in gorillas.

"It would be fun to really *know* some gorillas," I said. "To be able to touch them, and hang around with them every day."

My mom nodded.

"And George is nice," I said. "He cares about the gorillas."

Mom nodded again and said, "But . . ."

"But there's something too sad about it," I said. "Something depressing about how the gorillas looked at us."

My mom took her hand off the steering wheel and patted my knee.

"And anyway," I reminded her, "I'm going to be a singer."

When we got home, I hung around in the backyard sharing a cheese sandwich with Honey Bunny. We watched a gray lizard doing push-ups in the sun on the flagstones.

"I know this sounds gross," I said to Honey, "but if the garbage can was full of water *before* Mrs. Weston put the trap in it, then the raccoon would have had a faster death than if she filled it while he was in there. Wouldn't that make it less cruel?"

Honey concentrated on the sandwich.

"But that would mean it's okay to kill if you do it fast, and that doesn't sound right either, does it? But it *is* all right to kill to eat. Not just humans do that."

Honey turned away to watch a scrub jay at the bird feeder. The jay tipped his head, using one eye at a time to look for the sunflower seeds. He flicked all the other kinds of seeds to the ground.

"I know *you* don't kill anyone," I continued to Honey, "but lions do. They can't just eat lettuce and grass. And does killing to protect yourself include killing to protect your petunias, or your goldfish? Fancy, expensive goldfish? If a coyote came in our yard to eat you, wouldn't you expect me to protect you like Sweet Betsy protected her tall Shanghai rooster and old yellow dog?"

My song was on my mind all the time, because the concert was next Friday. I sang the last verse for Honey: " 'They swam the wide rivers and crossed the tall peaks, they camped on the prairies for weeks and for weeks. They fought off coyotes with musket and ball, and reached California in spite of it all.' "

My dad's voice came from right behind me. "If a coyote comes in our yard, I expect you to go indoors immediately. You can make noise to scare it away, but protect yourself first. Your rabbit is on her own. Nice singing, though."

My mom came outside with a garbage bag and the scissors. That meant she was going to hack away at Dad's hair and call it a haircut. Neither of them seemed to mind how peculiar these haircuts looked. They just acted pleased as punch at saving a few bucks—like they'd foiled an evil plot among the world's barbers to rob them.

Mom looked from Dad to me and said, "We have good news, Ava. We got someone to cover for us at the clinic over your spring break, and we are going to take some time off! How's that? A little family vacation. We can leave Friday night, right after your music program, if we get all our packing done."

"Cool!" I said. "Let's go to Mexico!"

"Well, we were thinking of Santa Barbara, actually."

Uh-oh, I thought. Santa Barbara meant the Perfect Taylors and their perfectly dreary condo that isn't even in bike riding distance to the beach.

I said, "Not Santa Barbara! Not Rita and Eli. Why do we have to do everything with them?" I knew I was whining, but I couldn't help it.

My mom kept clipping, but her back went straight. "The Taylors are like family to us," she said. "And you've been so mopey lately, we thought this would cheer you up."

"It won't," I said. "Rita and Eli make me sick. Especially Rita."

"That's just foolish," my mother said. Clip, clip, clip. "Rita is a lovely girl and she's been like a sister to you."

"Yeah, and how often do you take vacations

with *your* lovely sister?" I asked. I knew that was mean, but I wanted to be mean. My mom only saw her family at weddings and funerals, and not always then.

She got huffy. "We are doing this for *you*, Ava."

"Well, you should have asked me," I said and ran into the house, banging the screen.

My father called after me, "You get back here and apologize to your mother!"

I pretended I hadn't heard. At dinner my parents and I acted stiff with each other because I hadn't apologized for yelling at my mom, and they obviously hadn't cancelled our dreadful travel plans. I gave myself credit for my father's extra-horrendous haircut—living proof that I had rattled the haircutter.

After school on Thursday I took Ralph out for a walk. He and I never walked near Zinny's house anymore. That part of the subdivision could have grown scales and I wouldn't have known it. I tried not to care.

The Spring Program was tomorrow. I didn't want to remember how Zinny and I had fantasized about the talent scout in the audience. That seemed so long ago, and the memory hurt my chest. But the thoughts just seemed to come.

We used to say that when I was an incredibly

famous singer, Zinny would design my spectac-
ular costumes, with headdresses and masks that
would drive the audience crazy. Other singers and
movie stars would beg her to do their wardrobes,
and they'd offer her truckloads of money. But
she'd say, "Nah, thanks anyway," and smile very
sweetly.

Now I really hoped there would be a talent
scout, a record producer, *someone* in the audience
who would hear me sing and sweep me away to a
life of fame and fortune and friends.

I noticed two girls walking up the street toward
me. I knew at once it was Zinny and Suki and
boom, my heart started pounding. It was too late
to turn a corner, so I just marched on. Ralph
bounded ahead. I whistled for him to stop, but he
paid no attention.

Zinny darted across the street to escape Ralph.
Suki quickly followed her. Ralph was just about to
cross after them when I yelled, "Stop!" and he
miraculously obeyed.

"Get a leash for that beast!" Zinny yelled—the
first words she'd spoken to me since the whole
thing began.

"Or what?" I yelled back. "You'll kill him?"

Zinny stopped and stared at me from across the
street.

"You better not do it in front of Suki," I yelled,
"or her mom will report you."

Zinny looked at me with confusion. I could see her brain working. She turned and looked at Suki. Suki took two steps backward and said nothing. A car went by between us just then, so I didn't hear what anyone said, but then I saw Suki take another step backward.

I whistled for Ralph and continued to move down the street. I tried to walk calmly, head up, as if my heart was not racing. As if I wasn't suddenly completely sweaty. What if I was wrong? What if it wasn't Suki's mom who called Animal Protection but, somehow, Rita? Or what if it was some other person altogether who reported Mrs. Weston? It took all my strength to keep moving and not look back.

The next day was the last day of school before spring break. I looked up from the gorilla book I was reading at recess and I thought I saw Zinny send a little smile in my direction. But I wasn't sure. Other than that, the day passed like all the others—except for the butterflies in my stomach. The Spring Program was going to be that night, at 7:00.

When I got home from school, my mom presented me with my first pair of pantyhose—not tights, but clear stockings!

"Ta da!" she said. Then she held out a pink

razor and a can of shaving cream in her other hand and offered to teach me how to shave my legs! "You will get nicked, though," she said. "That's just part of life. I'm forty-two and I still cut myself."

Ralph came to watch and we all crowded into the bathroom. I sat on the counter with my foot in the sink.

"When you've had more practice," Mom said, "you'll be able to do it in the shower." Her face blotched up like she was going to cry and she said, "My baby is growing up." She hugged me and put kisses all over my face, smearing the front of her shirt with shaving cream.

Then she and I were squirting shaving cream at each other and laughing like hyenas. Ralph barked and snapped at the globs of shaving cream that flew through the air.

Afterward my legs felt tingly and perfectly smooth. I couldn't stop petting my shins, they felt so different.

My parents dropped me at school at 6:30, then went to look for a parking space. A lot of kids were already there, everyone wearing white shirts and dark pants or skirts. When Mr. Draper saw me, he called me over and pinned a red carnation to my shirt.

"For our soloist," he said.

Zinny brushed past me, then turned around

and looked me right in the eye. "Break a leg," she said, which in show-biz talk means good luck.

That was nice, right? Or did she mean break a leg like fall on my face and scream in pain? Before I could figure it out, she was gone.

We filed on to the bleachers. The blue curtains opened. The audience hushed. First the lights were too bright to see anything. Then Mr. Draper played the opening chords of the first song. I didn't have a chance to search out my parents, let alone figure out if any of the people out there looked like talent scouts.

Then we were singing, "'Grasshopper sittin' on the railroad tracks, singing polly wolly doodle all the day. . . .'" We sang the next three songs and I counted on my fingers behind my back. Two more until "Sweet Betsy from Pike."

The applause after "Clementine" stopped and Mr. Draper looked at me. He nodded his head. I filled my lungs with air. Then I opened my mouth and sang.

My heart beat so loud in my ears that I could hardly hear myself sing. When verse number one was over, everyone joined me on the "Sing too ra li, oo ra li, oo ra li ay." I imagined that surfing felt like this, being carried higher and higher on a wave. . . .

At the top of the wave I was alone again, singing

my second verse. I was calmer this time and I started having fun. Another wave swelled up with the chorus, and the third verse felt great. I knew I'd hit every note right on.

This is why I want to be a singer, I thought. It's not the excitement, it's when the nervousness calms down and the music comes up from my toes and fills my head, and flows out as easily as breathing. I wished the song had ten more verses.

The audience was applauding and Mr. Draper winked at me. We sang our finale, "This Land Is Your Land," and the audience sang along. Then the curtains closed and it was over.

I don't remember leaving the stage, but we must have because then we were in the corridor, being mobbed by parents. Then I was out the door and into the quiet dark, on the way to the car with my parents. They were happily gabbing away, but I felt myself start to sink. Of course all that stuff about a talent scout had just been a silly game. But to practice so hard and sing my very best, just to leave, alone with my parents. . . .

Suddenly I missed Zinny so badly that I felt all emptied out inside. Like that horrible feeling you get when you fall backward and have the wind knocked out of you. Or the feeling I had when my lizard Roll died: After I was all cried out, I was left feeling dry and hollow. It was just like that.

We stopped at home to load the suitcases and birds and crabs and rats and dog into our van. Honey was going to be on her own, like a regular wild rabbit, and Ralph was going to come with us to Santa Barbara, but the other animals would stay at the shelter. Ralph sat heavily on my lap and slobbered out the window. It was hard to stay entirely miserable with a big warm dog in my lap. But it was easy to stay somewhat miserable, dreading the next five days in stupid Santa Barbara.

When we got to the shelter to drop our pets and pick up the Taylors, the coyotes were howling, the sky was full of stars, and I heard the lion roar. I was just admitting to myself that I loved the shelter at night when Rita slid into the seat beside me and said, "I'm so sick of this place, I could scream!"

"What?" I asked, shocked that goody-goody Rita was actually complaining about something.

"Just take me somewhere, anywhere, that doesn't smell like animal urine!" Rita said.

I laughed.

Santa Barbara was nothing like I'd thought it would be. Rita was actually sort of fun.

The new Rita still did a lot more chores than I did. She was still, I thought, incredibly polite to our parents and patient with her brother. She helped fix meals and do dishes without being asked. And she still kept her things tidy as a pin, but something had definitely changed for the better.

She and I stood at the edge of the world, where the land runs out and the sea begins. The tide sucked the sand out from under our feet as Rita told me about wanting to set sail for Europe one day. Paris, Athens, Madrid. I had never ever suspected that Rita had hopes and dreams. How human!

When we were poking sticks into the embers of a campfire one night, I mentioned that Zinny and I used to tell each other ghost stories.

"Zinny, Zinny, Zinny!" Rita said. "I can't tell you how sick I am of hearing that name!"

My mouth fell open. Rita was jealous! Just like a real girl!

I liked throwing sticks into the surf for Ralph to fetch. I liked filling my pockets with shells to bring home for my crabs. It was nice being away from school—away from worrying about who I'd run into at the library or while walking the dog. But the most interesting part of spring break was witnessing the miracle of Rita coming to life.

I was sitting next to her in the van on the way home when she asked me if I'd ever done anything about the raccoon killer.

"No," I said. "Did you?"

"Did I what?" she asked.

"Did you tell anyone?"

Rita rolled her eyes. "No, I did not tattle on your precious Zinny. It was Zinny, wasn't it?"

"No," I said, "it was her mom."

When we got home, there were fourteen messages on our answering machine. I assumed they were the usual sick animals, so I didn't listen. I was outside dumping the sand out of my backpack and talking to Honey Bunny when my dad said, "Zinny called."

"Zinny called?" I was shocked. "What did she say?"

My dad shrugged. "I don't know, I'm just giving you the message."

"So, what was the message?" I almost shrieked.

He looked at me as if I'd grown horns. "Dad! This is important!"

"Well, excuse me," he said. "I didn't know I had to take notes. Ask your mother."

I ran inside. "Mom? What did Zinny say?" My mom put her hand over the phone and glared at me. "Shhhh," she hissed, "I'm on the phone!"

My dad had come up behind me. "Gregory's Lab, Nick, was hit by a car," he explained.

I know Nick, he's a great old yellow Labrador, and he has been a patient at the clinic forever, but ZINNY CALLED.

I stood around for what seemed like hours while my mom talked first to the clinic about how Nick was doing—which, from the look on her face, was pretty bad. Then she talked to Gregory to say how sorry she was that she'd been out of town.

I knew there was no getting through to her, and she probably skimmed over Zinny's message anyway, and my dad was hopeless, so I decided, what the heck. I put my shoes on and headed up the street to Zinny's house.

Would she be home? Would she be alone, or would Suki or Crystal be there? What if Mrs. Weston answered the door? What if my dad got it wrong and it wasn't Zinny who called? My feet took me closer and closer. What would I say? "Hi. Is your mom in jail?" At least I now knew for absolutely sure that Rita hadn't told anyone. . . .

There was Zinny's house. And there was her front door. I didn't have to knock. The door opened and Zinny stepped out.

"Hey," she said shyly.

"Hey, yourself," I said.

"I was a jerk," Zinny said.

"Yes," I said, "you were."

"A mean, stupid jerk."

"Septic pond scum," I agreed.

"Worse," Zinny said, smiling. "I'm so sorry, Ava."

"You *should* be sorry—way sorry," I said, smiling back, a little.

"So, can we just go back to being best friends and forget it ever happened?" Zinny asked. "Just pretend there was cosmic interference in our reception, a blip on our TV screen—and now the picture is suddenly and mysteriously restored?"

Zinny's voice wrapped around me like those old costume curtains, and it felt good. I wanted to beam myself back in time to when things were easy. But how would I ever trust her again? Couldn't she just turn against me sometime?

"You're not answering," Zinny said. "That's not good."

There were so many things I wanted to say, but none of them came out.

"Would it help if I begged?" Zinny asked. "Or if I whipped myself with chains? Walked on hot coals?"

"It would help if you explained," I said.

Zinny sighed. "I was afraid of that." She sat down on the step and I sat beside her. "I wish you'd picked the hot coals," she said.

"Well, maybe you could do the coals too," I said.

"This is going to sound so stupid, you'll hate me even worse," Zinny began. "But here goes. The truth, the whole truth, and nothing but the truth, so help me God." She took a deep breath. "Remember a long time ago," she said, "when your dad and my dad had a fight about your rabbit?"

I nodded.

"Well, starting then, I sort of began waiting for you to hate me. Waiting for you to think me and my whole family were idiots."

"What?" I asked.

"Well," said Zinny, "you never said *anything* about the rabbit thing."

"Neither did you."

"What could I say? I knew you wanted me to be different. You wanted me to go out to your animal shelter. You wanted me to like your rats, your clams—"

"Crabs," I said.

"Whatever. Your birds, your dog—your whole Noah's ark. I knew I wasn't who you wanted me to be."

"Wow! You were worried about that?" I shook my head in disbelief.

"And then, when you saw the trap in our yard, the look on your face was so . . . scary. I was pretty sure you already hated me. I kept waiting for you to *say* something about it, but you hardly said anything! You just pretended everything was normal."

"Why didn't *you* say something?" I asked.

Zinny shrugged. "I guess I was afraid to."

"Wow," I said a second time.

"So then, when those animal police came, it was like it was too late to talk," Zinny said. "I was sure that you'd told your parents, and your dad had reported my mom, because of what happened with Honey Bunny and the petunias. And it was my *mother* who got in trouble, because of you, I thought. I freaked out."

"And you never suspected Suki's mother?" I asked.

"Never."

One more "Wow!" slipped out of me. "So what happened when I blew Suki's cover?" I asked.

"Well, then *Suki* completely freaked out. I guess she'd planned on my just not speaking to you for the rest of my life, so I'd never learn the truth."

"Now are you not speaking to *her*?" I asked.

"I'm speaking to her," Zinny said. "It probably sounds even more stupid, but since I didn't like her as much as I liked you, I didn't have to hate her as much as I hated you."

I sat there shaking my head in wonder.

"But I never really *hated* you, Ava," Zinny said. "It was more like I was hiding from your hating me. Does that make any sense?"

It did make sense, in a twisty sort of way, and I told her so. "And what happened to your mom?"

"Nothing. The whole thing was dropped."

"I'm glad," I said.

"Really?" Zinny asked.

"Really."

We were still sitting on the front steps when the sun started to set spectacularly. "It's pretty," Zinny said.

"It's pollution," I said. "Another gift from our ancestors."

"Well, it's nice to know that it's not *our* fault," Zinny said. "We can like the colors without feeling guilty." Then she added, "And it wasn't Suki's fault that her mom snitched on my mom."

"No, but it *is* her fault that she let me take the blame," I said. "And it's your fault that you blamed me. It's not your fault that your mom did what she did to that raccoon, though," I said. "I never blamed you for that."

"Blame, blame, fault, fault, fault," Zinny said. "Listen to us!"

Mrs. Weston opened the front door. I wasn't sure how to react, so I didn't. She came out carrying two identical, carefully arranged plates. Each had two triangles of baloney sandwich, four grapes, one slice of orange, and a glass of milk balanced exactly in the middle. I knew it was a peace offering and I said, "Thank you."

Zinny and I promised to talk about the stuff that worried us from then on. And we vowed not to let anything our parents did ruin our friendship.

The next day we summoned Suki and Crystal to a secret ceremony up in Zinny's room. We pulled a blanket over all our heads and joined hands in the center.

Zinny put on a very serious voice and said, "Repeat after me. We can't help what parents we got."

"'We can't help what parents we got,'" Suki, Crystal, and I said in unison.

"We can't help loving the parents we got," said Zinny, and we three repeated it.

"But none of us are responsible for what our parents do," Zinny said.

Suki, Crystal, and I chanted after her.

"And we do solemnly swear and promise never to blame each other for stuff that's not our fault," Zinny said.

"Amen!" added Suki. And we did a secret handshake.

Then we tromped downstairs and stood stiffly around the fishpond, trying to think of more sacred oath stuff, until Crystal said, "Remember that guy with his pants slipping down his butt?"

We all laughed and the ceremony was over.

Two weeks later I made my Rwanda presentation, and it was great. I put my gorilla information into a song and sang it to the tune of "Twinkle, Twinkle, Little Star." Here's how it went:

> I had my first child at ten.
> At fourteen I'll breed again.
> I live with a silverback.
> He's the leader of our pack.
> All the rest of us are girls.
> And our babies, cute as pearls.

> It takes lots of leaves and twigs
> To grow bodies quite this big.
> That's why we need lots of trees.
> Get your own trees, if you please.

If Rwanda can't stay green,
I will never more be seen.

I don't know if anyone in the class cared about my facts, but the gorilla costume Zinny made for me was a huge hit. And I ended up letting Melinda and Suki sing backup. They each held tree branches and swayed in rhythm, singing "oooooh," and "doo-ap, diddly doo."

Then one day in my backyard, Zinny and I heard rustling in the bushes. We climbed off the hammock and looked. A tiny face peeked out from under the bush, and then a second face with miniature bunny ears and a twitchy nose.

The next moment, baby bunnies the size of furry tennis balls came bubbling and rolling out into the yard. I counted three, four, six of them! Hop, hop, hop. All different combinations of colors, from Honey's honey color to the speckled gray of our local wild rabbits.

Honey had no voice to announce, "Look what I made! Here they are!" But she did look proud as she nuzzled my hand for a treat.

I called to my parents and my dad stuck his head out the door. "I'm a grandma!" I shrieked. "Honey's babies are here! Can I pick one up?"

"She wants you to," my dad said. "She brought

them to you." He laughed and disappeared back inside.

I scooped up a gray one. It nestled in the palm of my hand and didn't act one bit afraid. I was petting it and cooing when Zinny put out her hands. I was totally shocked, but I handed her the baby.

Zinny held it just right, gently but firmly against her body. She said, "Ooooooh, it's so cute! It's so soft! Look at its itty-bitty tail!" She held it up to cuddle against her cheek, then said, "Can I keep it?"

"We could ask my parents if you could keep it here," I said. "With Honey."

"But it would be mine, right?" Zinny asked. "My pet?"

"All yours, Zinny." I smiled. "Absolutely."